RECCE PATROL

Strike Force Falklands
4

RECCE PATROL

ADAM HARDY

Macdonald

A Macdonald Book

First published in Great Britain in 1985
by Macdonald & Co (Publishers) Ltd
London & Sydney

British Library Cataloguing in Publication Data

Hardy, Adam
    Recce patrol.—(Strike Force Falklands; 4)
    Rn: Kenneth Bulmer   I. Title   II. Series
    823'.914[F]   PR3552.U46
    ISBN 0 356 12007 4

Printed in Great Britain by
Redwood Burn Limited, Trowbridge, Wiltshire
Bound at the Dorstel Press

Macdonald & Co (Publishers) Ltd
Maxwell House
74 Worship Street
London EC2A 2EN

A BPCC plc Company

Chapter One

'I thought they said there was no Argie for ten miles around?'

'That's what they said.'

'Well, they didn't tell those two up there.'

The voices whispered from mouth to ear.

Stretched out flat as a limpet against the peaty ground, Jack Dexter could plainly see, up ahead against the star glitter, the two round Argie helmets. The sheer crassness of the situation precipitated these unnecessary words. At Dexter's side, Punch Fuller could simply have hand-pressed a message had any signal been necessary.

With the scent of the peat in his nostrils and the dank feel to the air that signalled dawn was not far off, Dexter realized Punch felt the same sense of screaming frustration as he did. Here in West Falkland they had a simple job to do, with not an Argentine soldier within miles, someone had goofed and so the situation *was* normal: all fouled up.

There was just the one task to execute.

The four-man patrol of Major Dan Granville's Special Strike Force had been choppered in, abseiled down with their kit, and had marched just far enough to make it up over the ridge and get under cover before dawn. And now they'd run slap bang into a stupid Argie lookout.

For such a powerfully-built and barkily-tough a man, Jack Dexter moved with precise control in every action.

5

He and Punch Fuller removed their humping great jaguar packs without straining unduly, without noise, and swiftly. The pack joined the LAW and the sacks on the peat.

The helmeted heads of the sentries turned from time to time, and the flicker of a match could be distinctly heard spluttering in the windless night.

A cigarette lit up, and then another.

There were only two sentries, so they didn't have to worry about the three-match superstition. On such a silent night the men of SSF were not going to compromise their operation by shooting.

Punch stretched his hand out behind his buttocks and Lance Corporal Smith put his fingers up against Punch's.

'Stay.' That was command enough.

The other lance jack in the patrol remained silent and unmoving. His name, too, was Smith.

Low and lethal, Dexter and Punch started up the slope in pursuit of the Argies.

Lance Corporal Sidney Smith stared up after the two deadly shapes silhouetted against the stars, and before he had time to blink they disappeared. The drabness and darkness of the scene, lit only by the high glitter of the stars and those two idiot cigarettes, had no effect on Smith's nerves. Like all the others of the hand-picked bunch called Strike Force, his nerves were tidily packaged, tied up, labelled and stowed away for the duration.

Sidney Smith, known as SS for obvious reasons, eased the straps of his jaguar pack. He'd sooner be up there getting on with it, rather than just waiting for Punch and the Joker to finish up.

At his side, Lance Corporal Alf Smith shared exactly the same thoughts. He was known as Dingle. No one knew why. The truth was that many of the sobriquets used in Strike Force as recognition names, security-proof

6

rapid-reaction names, had no rational explanation. Maybe, deep down, there lurked subconscious reasons why certain blokes were called certain names. Dingle stared up after Punch and the Joker, and sweated out the wait.

For WOII Arthur Fuller, the relief of being able to get into a fight came to him sweetly. In addition, the reaction charged him up, gave him the kind of boost he was well aware he craved. He'd argued the merits and demerits of being that way with Captain Tom Burnaby, and neither man could agree.

If these two stupid Argies got in the way of the job that had to be done, then that was their hard luck.

Negotiating the slope was not difficult, the tricky part would come higher up. The whole lay of the land here struck Punch Fuller as odd. To their rear a ridge of rocks stuck up like a hog's back; they were currently negotiating a peaty section, and a narrow and steeply-rocky gorge loomed ahead of them, at the crest of which stood the two Argie sentries.

Away to the left a pebbly beach offered no real outflanking route, and the track to the right would have baffled a goat. So it was straight up the middle.

Jack Dexter reached the same unsatisfactory conclusion. Neither man made much noise; inevitably, a tiny scrape of boot leather slithered into the night air; but they did not gasp or pant, and those Argies wouldn't have a ghost of a chance of hearing the men of Strike Force until it was far, far too late.

Higher up, the wedge-shape of the gorge narrowed so that the peat became a mere strip. Without thinking about it, Dexter allowed Punch to take the lead. He was in command of the patrol. The fact that he was a warrant officer class two and Dexter was a sergeant had nothing to do with it.

Up ahead now, there was no sign of those big, clumsy

round Argie helmets.

Punch halted and Dexter felt the CSM's hand pressing signals.

'Wait.'

Dexter remained fast as Punch continued, flat as an eel, up the track.

Punch Fuller stood six foot three, with a frame to match, and his face, once described by an awed girl he'd been chatting up at a disco as 'Hawk-like', held a light demonic in its intensity. He favoured a thick black moustache and his chin would have sunk a battleship, yet he wriggled up the slope like a snake, flat and unseen – and silently.

Near the crest of the gorge he halted. There was no sign of the Argies. His tiger-striped face peered slowly this way and that; but there was no chance the two sentries could be on this side of the saddle. They must have sloped off after finishing whatever they'd been here for and dropped down the opposite side.

His Dispersed Pattern Material anorak, which in daylight blended him in with his surroundings, could do little at night; his tiger-striped face and blackened metal equipment fittings reflected no starlight. He had no doubt that he could sneak up to the saddle and look over without much risk of being spotted.

As he started off again he reflected that he was well-known for his taciturn nature. He seldom spoke and what he said was to the point. So why had he been drooling off at the mouth back there? What the hell the Joker would make of it, Punch suddenly realized he didn't want to know.

Jack Dexter, instead of ruminating on his comrade's odd lapse into garrulity, was staring hard up at the gorge and trying to do the near-impossible. He was trying to see a member of Strike Force sneaking up on an enemy sentry.

As he expected, he saw no sign of Punch.

Presently a head appeared over the rocks against the starlight and an arm waved. The signal unmistakably meant: 'Come on!'

Making sure everything was still attached to him, Dexter wriggled along up the gorge, keeping low, making no noise, a lethal member of Strike Force. Punch chose to wear a rolled-up balaclava, and that was the shape of the head Dexter had seen. If he'd noticed a round Argie helmet he would have been totally astonished.

He was surprised when he got up with Punch to find the CSM was alone. There were no dead Argies in sight.

Speaking in that low whisper that just carried, he said: 'Well?'

'Scarpered.'

'What the hell were they on sentry go for, then?'

'Search me.'

The torch Punch dug out had been rigged with a quick-action trigger. He aimed it down the track and signalled.

'Dit, dit, dit. Dit, dit, dah, dit. S.F.'

After that he sent: 'Dah, dit, dah. K.'

Down-slope, the two Smiths, SS and Dingle, picked up the rapier-thin flicker of directed light.

'Bloody nerve!' SS groped around for Punch's kit.

'Yeah. Wouldn't come on net so's we could tell him to stuff hisself.' Dingle grabbed Dexter's kit.

'Nah,' said SS, thoroughly disgruntled. 'Make two trips. I ain't shifting this bloody lot in one go.'

'Check.'

With that they started off, leaving a sizeable chunk of their two comrades' kit strewn over the peaty ground.

Dexter squinted back down-slope.

'Didn't work,' he said. 'Not likely – what, all that kit!'

'Poofters,' said Punch, simply because that was

expected of him as one of the roughest, hairiest, strongest fellows in Strike Force. At around a hundred pounds each to be carried, no one in their right mind was going to hump double that.

The two Smiths came up in ominous silence.

'I'll go,' said Dexter.

He and SS went off down-slope. The stars no longer held that icy-bright sharpness and the faintest tremors of a breeze stirred against his cheeks. With the dawn would come mist. Well, that suited Strike Force when they were sneaking around in the other fellow's back yard, but once in position on this obbo job they needed good visibility.

SS pointed to the strewn kit. 'I'll take Punch's.'

'Be my guest.'

Punch Fuller carried far more than anybody else.

Helping SS get the monstrous pack onto his back and hefting him upright, Dexter killed a smile. As a member of Strike Force he sometimes felt he had far too strong a sense of humour in ways far removed from that of his comrades. They all liked a joke, the cruder and bloodier the better, at times; Dexter wasn't called the Joker for nothing.

When they reached the top of the saddle they dropped flat and wriggled over the exposed section, fast. Down-slope they joined up with the others and the kit was repositioned. Ahead lay an open stretch, still bounded by terrible terrain, and the ridge that was their objective hard-edged against the sky. That sky held the tiniest flush of dove-pink. Mist began to seep into the air.

'Leg it,' said Punch, and started off with his enormous strides.

The others followed. Selected by Major Dan Granville and trained hard for Strike Force, they kept up. No one was going to fall out. This little hack wouldn't disturb a fly. The ridge neared.

The mist proved a wonderful comfort to Dexter as he

plodded on after Punch. If those two Argies who'd scarpered were scanning their backtrail from the ridge ahead they must, despite all the patrol's expertise, spot them eventually like this. The mist gave them a chance to get up close before sticking everything into the earth and doing a stalk.

Up ahead Punch carried his silenced Sterling ready for action. A tick of worry fluttered in Dexter's mind. Old Punch, now, he really liked to get stuck in. If he'd shot those two poor devils of Argies, instead of trying to get in close for a spot of hand-to-hand, Dexter wouldn't be sweating about hostile eyes watching them right now.

Still, Dexter had too much respect for Punch's sheer professionalism to fault him a hundred per cent. There could have been more Argies on the reverse slope of the saddle. On such a quiet night, even the *plop-plop* of the silenced Patchett might carry.

No. He'd go along with old Punch all the way. They'd really changed the fish and chip industry, though, hadn't they? With this comforting thought warming him he followed on in Punch's footsteps.

There was, in God's truth, little for him to feel comfort in on this job.

They'd really been handed the sticky end this time. When the orders were handed out Punch had said, 'We've been shafted!'

When it was pointed out to him, patiently, that one of the most important missions that Special Strike Force performed was recon, observation and intelligence, Punch, brushing up that heavy black moustache, had replied, 'But we're a *Strike* Force!'

There was no argument. Number Three Wing of Strike Force would land in West Falkland. They would check out certain beaches to see if they were suitable for landing craft, what the beach exits were like, if they were overlooked by useful spots for Argie positions and

11

generally report on the feasability of the Task Force making a landing.

The fact that they'd trained for this work, as they'd trained for an amazing variety of other work, could not mollify Punch Fuller. He felt personally affronted that Numbers One and Two Wings were going to have all the fun and Number Three would be left out. As for Number Four, they were weeping hot tears into their pints.

'No one knows where the Task Force is going to land, Punch,' Tom Burnaby told him. 'We're headed for East Falkland. If the Task Force go ashore in West, then you'll catch it.'

'And,' amplified Smyjo, passing a finger across his guardsman's moustache, 'wherever the Task Force goes ashore, eventually all Strike Force will be involved.'

So Punch had had to like it and lump it.

Sergeant Dennis Underhill, known for perfectly logical reasons as Deadly Dennis, giving his rifle a quite unnecessary polish in so immaculate a weapon, commented, 'We're floating over the oggin at the mercy of the pussers. Who knows where they'll wind up?'

Someone threw a boot at him, and an interesting brawl developed. However all that had happened soon after they'd left Portsmouth, and now Strike Force was scattered over the islands, and Punch's patrol of Number Three Wing were experiencing a few trifling yet infuriating delays in their job.

Jack Dexter was certain of one thing. If a likely target showed up, Punch would go for it bald-headed.

Approaching the ridge in the lee of which they intended to set up shop, they adopted standard procedure and stalked up the last metres of the slope. The mist thickened steadily and the light could be imagined to be improving, a pale anaemic lightening around them.

Punch's broad hand motioned. 'Stop.'

The three men waited silent and unmoving as the CSM wriggled his way forward. His jaguar pack and kit had come off with that lizard-like sinuousness of movement practiced a thousand times – often with live rounds whistling a foot or so overhead.

A black and panther like shape, he would be seen as a highly sinister and unpleasant sort of antagonist for any poor Argie conscript to find himself up against. Number Three Wing of Strike Force had been warned that there might be elements of the Argentine Special Forces around. 'The good old Buzo Tactico' as Smyjo, the force's Intelligence officer, had referred to them. Then he'd added, in his serious voice, 'They're reputedly a tough bunch. So don't underestimate them.'

Well, if there were any up there with their funny woollen hats, they'd be grist to the mill for Punch Fuller – that was Jack Dexter's considered opinion.

A brief arm wave signalled the three waiting men forward. Dexter leading, they moved up to the crest of the ridge – and, still, they proceeded quietly and cautiously. Punch vanished over the far side.

This was leadership Punch understood, as taught by Major Dan Granville. Leadership from the front. Get up there and get stuck in.

Dexter reached the crest in the same instant that a rifle shot cracked starkly from the rocks. He leapt forward filled with blazing anger. Someone had botched it.

Just down-slope of him a bunch of indistinct figures were milling about. He saw a body fly up into the air and topple away, arms and legs flailing, and heard a shriek of agony. Dexter rushed down and forward, swinging his rifle up into line.

He saw it all with distinct and horrifying clarity.

Punch was down. He'd taken three of them already, but two more poised above him swung up their rifles.

13

As Dexter, yelling blue bloody murder, charged forward, a rifle butt smashed towards Punch's unprotected head.

Chapter Two

Dexter shot off a whole mag.

He didn't hesitate. He sprayed the 5.56mm rounds at the group, aiming over Punch's prostrate body, and saw one of the men who was attempting to bash Punch's brains out stagger back, the tumble-rounds swathing across his chest. The other one, hit and screaming, brought his rifle butt down.

In the noise and confusion Dexter could not hear the soggy thump of that blow. But he could sense it, sense the devastating smash of the rifle butt against the back of Punch's head.

In the next second Dexter was down there, in among them, and lashing about with his rifle.

He was vaguely aware of SS and Dingle there with him; but he concentrated on getting his legs astride Punch's prostrate form and of killing anyone who tried to harm his comrade.

Two of the enemy soldiers tried to run for it. The Smiths took one each, their SLRs cracking out with a brief and staccato bark. The soldiers tumbled over.

Dexter didn't bother to glare around him. He could leave all that had to be done immediately to SS and Dingle. He bent to Punch.

The CSM lay there, and the blood beneath the rolled balaclava looked black and greasy. He breathed with a rasping snore, stertorously, as though rolling drunk.

Dexter's veins were filled with what felt like ice-water. Gingerly, he touched Punch's cranium.

The bone felt spongy and soft, and he snatched his hand away as though he had been stung.

'Gently,' he said, admonishing himself.

SS said in a rasp: 'Can't stay here now.'

'No.'

'Punch okay?' Dingle stood poised, alert, looking all around and not at the CSM.

'No. Skull's bashed in. He'll have to be ...'

'Yeah.'

'At least he's still alive.'

'Weren't there rocks along the beach?' demanded SS.

'Let's leg it, then. Help me with Punch.'

Working rapidly, they spread out a camouflaged poncho and put the injured man upon it with all the care a mother might lavish upon a newborn baby. Punch's face looked sunken in. Dexter and Dingle took the front corners, and SS the rear of the poncho where Punch's legs and boots drew into the hammock-like sag.

'We'll leave his kit and the wireless.' Dexter licked his lips. His eyes were white halfmoons in the tiger-striped face. 'Come back for 'em soonest.'

'Check.'

'Let's get moving.'

They did not bother with the enemy soldiers. The mist might be dropping down now; daylight was approaching and there would be other enemy soldiers out there who'd heard the shooting. They'd come to investigate. Dexter, as he ran in as smooth a rhythm as he could manage opposite Dingle, worried about the wireless. That was their link with HQ and the only method they had for telling them what the hell was going on.

His guess was that the party they'd stumbled on were an advance post. Their main body could be anywhere. Say they'd heard the shooting – it might take them quite a time to sort out what was going on. Correction – what had gone on. He moved with sure and purposeful speed, knowing that SS and Dingle would pace him.

The rocks along the beach were an unknown quantity; they had to find shelter, and soon.

Punch's snorting gulps of air were distressing. Looking down, Dexter noted Punch's condition, guessed he'd probably suffered a depressed fracture, and cursed and cursed the uselessness of it all.

The sound of the sea gave some slight reassurance. They got in among the rocks and Dingle snapped out: 'Cave.'

They didn't have much option. The cave offered shelter. The entrance, partially masked by a tumble of stones, led to a largish space, pebbly-floored and around eight foot in height. Here they deposited Punch.

'Dingle, you stay with him. SS, strip off. Let's go.'

They dumped their massive loads, kept hold of their rifles, and started back. They moved fast and kept low, and their eyes ceaselessly scoured in every direction for the first sight of opposition.

The light in the sky now looked like sheep-dip. Objects possessed a strange luminosity, and appeared ghost like, strewn boulders looked hollow and as if negatives of holes. The breeze began to get up as the mist writhed about them, and the feeling of cold, which they pushed away, clamped down despite the coming of daylight.

Nothing appeared to have taken place at the crest line. They snatched up Punch's kit, Dexter swinging the enormous pack and its strapped-on bits and pieces onto his back. SS took up the wireless. With a last quick look around, they started back for the cave on the beach.

What, as Andy would say, a monumental cock-up!

The job had to be done. If this Strike Force patrol merely reported that the beaches they were assigned to recce were useless, that was positive information. The marine major who'd sussed out the various Falklands Islands beaches a few years ago was a marvel and his information priceless; now the men of Strike Force had to help other Special Forces patrols to determine on the final beach for the landing.

This cave they'd found was a fine place to hole up in under normal circumstances. The trouble was that the Argies knew the Brits were around and they'd come looking. In this situation the cave wouldn't do.

When they reached the cave and ducked down into the dark interior, they discovered that Dingle had fastened a bandage around Punch's head. The big CSM lay flat on his back, head supported, unconscious and looking awful; but at least his breathing was normal.

'Well?'

'He took a nasty whack, Joker. But I don't think his skull is busted.'

'Nah,' said SS. 'Built like a brick ...'

Dexter knelt on the shingle and stared at Punch.

'We'll have to carry him and the essential kit. Stash the rest somewhere. We can't stay here long.'

That was pure commonsense, but it rankled.

'What a foul up,' said Dingle, strapping up his valise.

'SS – go and keep your eyeballs peeled outside.'

Dexter turned back as SS went off silently and bent again to Punch.

Somehow or other – and Dexter wasn't at all sure quite in what direction his thoughts were leading – he could see that all was a consequence of the way Strike Force operated. Major Dan Granville, referred to as the major, or the Old man, led from the front. He expected his subordinates to do the same. Had there been two of them up there on the saddle, on the crest of the rocks, ready to leap down like panthers ... Well, no good could come of wishful thinking.

Not wasting any more time, mentally he began to run through a list of what they needed to take with them and what they could, reluctantly, leave. The LAWs could go. It was hardly likely that they'd run into any Argentine armour here on West Falkland; the rocket launchers had their own uses apart from their anti-armour capacities, the reason they'd been lugged along in the first place.

The Scimitar wireless in its carrying straps would have to be taken along. With that they could contact HQ. The marvel of the thing was the way it wobbled up and down the frequencies at random, making interception if not impossible, virtually so. Rumour had it, according to Tom Burnaby, that the English were developing a programme to intercept and read the signals from a wave-oscillating set. Bloody marvellous, if true, was Dexter's comment.

Their own pocket Scimitars were essential. Their weapons, too – Punch's silenced Sterling, his own bullpup Personal Weapon, and the two Smith's SLRs. Grub would have to be carted along. The people who graduated to the world of Strike Force were hard men, inured to privation, able to go for long periods on practically nothing. All the same, they had to eat something.

A few grenades might come in useful; but they could leave the plastic. As he sorted it all out, aware of Punch lying there looking like a bloody corpse, and Dingle clearly concerned over his own efforts at first-aid, Jack Dexter realized that he was in a pig of a situation.

He was standing with his own poncho gripped in his fists when SS stuck his head around the corner of the cave and said, 'Visitors. From the noise they're making they sound like a company. But I expect it's only a coupla them out to relieve themselves.'

Before the thought was fully formed the decision was made.

Dexter rammed his pack up against the poncho's edge,

pinning it to the rock. SS whistled into action instantly, hauling out his own poncho and spreading it over the upper section of the hole, letting it hang in shadowed folds. Outside, the mist drifted dankly.

Dingle's whisper ghosted to Dexter.

'Bottom left.'

'Well, bung us your …'

But Dingle's poncho was already in his fists and being lapped up to cover the last remaining gap. From outside, so Dexter hoped, the ponchos in their untidy layering, would look like a mere section of rock. The black hole of the cave should be entirely hidden.

That was the theory.

He found a tiny chink and glued an eyeball to it.

Well, it was daylight out there, such as it was. The mist ought to be gone soon. The sound of the approaching Argentines rattled against the rocks and attenuated in the dank air. Dexter did not move.

Quietly, Dingle slid back to check on Punch. The CSM's breathing was now shallow, and when Dingle touched his face the skin was icy cold. All the members of Strike Force had received medic training, which differed somewhat from standard first-aid. Indeed, it had to in the special circumstances which might require an injured man to march and function, when correct first-aid treatment insisted he rest and not be moved until the ambulance arrived. The stertorous breathing exhibited by Punch earlier on had caused Dingle to believe the CSM had sustained compression of the brain. Thankfully, there had been no sign of that tell-tale flushing of the face, or of bleeding from the nose or ears. Both pupils had also been the same size.

Dingle began to believe that Punch might be in better shape than he dared hope.

He turned away, picking up his rifle, and went to join Dexter at the cave mouth.

Dexter said, 'Can't see the blighters. The mist is still thickish.'

'Can hear 'em, though.'

'Yes.'

Dingle wedged himself alongside SS and found his own chink in the overlapping ponchos.

The tendrils of mist swirling and contorting away like spider silk gave the dreary scene an elfin beauty. The beat of the sea susurated out of sight, its waves lapping against one of the beaches they had to check out for the Task Force. A limpid and pallidly shadowless light hung over the rocks. In Dexter's nostrils the dank smell of the sea and the close confines of the cave brought back memories. He was sure the mist was easing and clearing. Objects stood out in sharper detail.

There was no need for words.

The first of the enemy patrol hove in sight, anoraks bulging, round helmets not gleaming but hard against that milky light. They were picking their way along the pebbles and boulders above the beach. Dexter counted five of them, with indistinct figures aft of the first group just moving forward, to take up in their turn the black silhouettes of hostiles.

Most of their rifles were slung. A couple of them in front carried SMGs. Dexter's breathing grew very small.

No sound came from the three men at the mouth of the cave, hidden behind the poncho camouflage. The Argentine patrol moved across their line of vision. The white splotchy twitch as faces turned towards the rocks, and away, caused no tremor in Dexter. He was confident the Argies wouldn't spot the camouflaged cave. After all, they were strangers around here, weren't they?

If only the stupid bastards who were their masters had had the sense not to try to steal something that wasn't theirs, this little charade wouldn't have had to be played out, and Punch Fuller wouldn't be lying back there with

21

a damned great bash on the head. Dexter cursed it all as he waited, ready for what might happen.

What did happen caught him on the hop – he just wasn't ready for that ...

The main group of Argentine soldiers passed directly before the hidden mouth of the cave.

In only a few moments the rest would follow and they'd be gone – and bad cess to 'em.

The feel of the little bullpup in his fists, the sense of the isolation of this place, the thought that the cave was pressing down and choking him, the worry over Punch and the problem of how to carry out their assigned mission, these matters weighed on Jack Dexter so heavily that he felt he could spit six-inch nails. What a foul up!

The Argentinians were passing, were drawing away, the leaders already merging mistily with the dank atmosphere.

At Dexter's back a growly voice hiccoughed, spat, and then burst out in a bull roar that rattled against the cave's walls and shook the hanging ponchos.

'What the hell's going on! Where am I? Where's that bastard who hit me?'

Dexter whirled, aghast.

Punch staggered up, arms flailing, bellowing in that horrendous parade-ground roar.

'I'll have him! I'll have him for breakfast and spit out the pips!'

SS and Dingle, in unison, cracked out: 'They heard him!' and: 'Here they come!'

Chapter Three

Punch Fuller understood precisely what was going on in a single all-encompassing glare. Instantly, he knew what was happening. His head did not hurt and he felt roaring fit and ready to rip up anything in his way.

What a bunch of wallies! He'd been knocked out and they'd dragged him here and then they'd hidden. Couldn't be more than half a dozen Argies out there, waiting to be chopped.

The Sterling in his fists, Punch charged at the entrance, cleared the hanging ponchos aside with a savage sweep, and belted out, looking for targets.

Big round helmets, padded anoraks – yes, there they were, all lined up and heading this way – targets!

He let rip with a controlled burst, scything into the approaching group of hostiles. Some fell, and he cut back in a return swathe of gunfire.

There was a wisp of mist encircling the area which gave an interesting added dimension to the action. As the hostiles ran in towards him from the shreds of mist they changed from vague and phantom figures into hard-edged enemy, prime targets. Some of them started to shoot back, and he sliced a savage burst towards the spots of flame, and yelled, 'Come on, you wallies! Let's have you!'

Jack Dexter watched what Punch was doing in horrified disbelief.

The big fellow had been knocked flat, out like a light, helpless. And here he was, raging and roaring and getting stuck in!

All Dexter could do was pelt outside after Punch swing his Personal Weapon into line and start shooting. The harder smacking discharges of the two SLRs alongside told him that SS and Dingle had reached the same pragmatic conclusion.

The first inquisitive reaction of the Argentines to Punch's bellows disappeared under the onslaught of the four weapons. The soldiers fell if they were shot, or ran if they were seized by blind panic, or tried to fling themselves into cover. The raking accuracy of the British shooting sought out the hostiles in crevices between the rocks, behind boulders, shot them up as they fled.

'Case-bound idiots!' raged Punch, sending the last of his magazine into a group trying to tumble pell-mell into a tangled sprawl of boulders.

There was no need to issue orders like: 'Cease fire!' and: 'Take cover!'

The men of Strike Force melted back into the fallen boulders alongside the cave mouth. One instant they were on their feet shooting; the next there was no sign of them.

Some shots had splattered against the rock-face at their backs and chips of stone had flown about in a nasty way; none of the Brits was hit.

Dexter gulped a breath of damp air.

'You all right, Punch?'

It was a fatuous question, Dexter knew that well enough; but it was a question that had to be asked.

Punch said: 'A crack on the head, boyo? No trouble.'

Dingle, sensibly, said nothing.

SS said, 'You took an awful hard crack, Punch.'

'Head like a steel coconut, boyo.'

Dexter didn't like the sound of all this one little bit.

What he knew about bangs on the head might be entirely pragmatic, and gained from painful experience; he remembered the feel of Punch's skull, the greasy blood, the way the big CSM had looked when they'd carted him into the cave.

He knew damn well they'd not heard the last of Punch's knock on the head, no matter what the big fellow was saying.

The Argies kept their heads down. Some of them loosed off a few rounds, but the Brits ignored this random musketry. Let the poor devils stand up and try to charge in and that would be the time to return the fire.

This idea displeased Dexter.

Cloaking his unease in an old old joke, he said quietly to Punch, 'If they bring up three and fourpence we're likely to get pinned here.'

'Not on your Nelly, Joker! We'll blow 'em apart and take off.'

'The sooner the better, then.'

A voice lifted out across the beach. The Spanish shrilled in with excitement loading every word. All Dexter could make out with his rough-and-ready Costa Brava package holiday Spanish was that the Argies wanted them to surrender.

He picked out *rendir* and *abandonar* and *rendicion*. It all hung together, for he could understand Spanish far better than he could speak it.

Thinking he'd probably got it all wrong, he yelled back: '*De ningun modo.*'

'What's that, Joker?'

'Told him no.'

'Tell him to stuff himself.'

Dexter remembered the time when a sink was bunged up in the hotel and Patsy, trying to wash her hair, had just about done her nut instead. The Spanish plumber from the hotel staff had rambled on something about *atorar.* He tried it, anyway, and quite expected the Argies across the way to laugh at his efforts. Then he sobered up. They had dead and wounded comrades and they were not in a laughing frame of mind.

Trouble was, as a member of Strike Force and thus expected to be fluent in a couple of languages and able to get by in a couple more, he was competent in Russian and Arabic, could cope in German, and everybody knew French, anyway – but his Spanish was strictly of the listening and not speaking variety.

That Patsy had been a bit of a handful too, in more ways than one. The plumber had kept about half an eye on the sink and the other one and a half on what Patsy was showing. Her hair, dripping wet, and bound up in a towel piled on her head, gave her a statuesque look she normally did not possess. She'd only been wearing a pair of lilac coloured briefs to wash her hair, and she didn't give a damn that the rest of her sun-bronzed body was on display.

Soap got into her eyes, and she was savage.

By the time the plumber had used his suction cup and cleared the sink, Dexter was just about past it. Just in time, the sink was unblocked, the plumber let himself out with a liquid and meaningful glance back, and Dexter was free to leap on Patsy.

Naturally, she squealed; but then she realized that she was in the mood too, and got down to business on the bed. Dexter could still feel the warmth and the softness of her, despite all the others, and her lips were marvels of osculatory magnificence, ready to suck him dry. By the time they'd finished – neck and neck – and Patsy decided to go back to washing her hair, Dexter had gone through the mill.

That was the kind of mill he'd go through any time – well, almost any time, witness poor little Yvonne.

The Argies started shouting again, and Dexter roused

himself from carnal thoughts of Patsy and the way her lilac briefs clung to her, apparently resisting genuine efforts at removal – and both of them trying, too – and listened to what was being yelled.

He said: 'They reckon, near as I can figure, we've no chance. Just pack it in and come out with our hands up.'

'We'll come out, and with our hands up,' said Punch in his evil voice. 'They'll be up them, the narners.'

This patrol of Strike Force had accomplished the task which it had been set. There were Argies around. If whoever made the final decision eventually decided to put the lads of the Task Force ashore here, then they would be aware of the potential opposition. That information had to be wirelessed back to HQ as a top priority.

Because Major Dan Granville's people had the inestimable blessing of being equipped with Scimitar wirelesses in place of the ubiquitous army Clansmen series of sets, and because they had a rear link permanently manned, in theory, they could call up HQ when they wished and not at pre-set timings.

Dexter decided that Punch was not himself. The CSM appeared inflated, elated, suffused with elan. That was a good thing in normal circumstances; right now Dexter harboured the direst suspicions that the crack on the head had done deep and nasty things to Punch.

He said, 'Dingle – get on to HQ. Tell 'em.'

'Check.'

Punch looked around, his enormously powerful face, craggy, moustached, thin of lip and mean of eye, regarded Dexter and Dingle.

Then he said, 'Yeah, sure. Tell HQ, Dingle.'

Without waiting for another assent, Dingle got on the set and called HQ.

What Dexter would have liked to do, something which was quite impossible in the circumstances, was call HQ

27

for a Casevac chopper. He wanted Punch out of here and in the sick bay where a proper doctor could take a careful look at him. But no helicopter was going to whirr in here, fitted for casualty evacuation, and lift Punch out.

The Argies might be all mouth, and of dubious value apart from the specialists, yet they'd shoot down a chopper quick enough if one was foolish enough to fly in during daylight.

'Right,' said Dingle, closing up the set. 'HQ wants the next beach in the bag.'

About to comment weakly that that was easier said than done, Dexter's words were blown away by Punch's cheerful *sotto-voce* roar.

'Righto, my old son! Then let's get to it!'

Dexter had to say, 'We've got until nightfall. The schedule specifically allowed for that time –'

'Nonsense! Joker! What the hell's got into you?'

'Do what?'

'Them Argies out there – nothing. A handful. A few clips up their arses and they'll run. I tell you, boyo, we'll get started right away.'

Usually taciturn, Punch Fuller was in the habit of getting things done, and his optimism in the face of all kinds of obstacles had brought him success many times in his eventful life. Jack Dexter knew that. He knew that he shared much of Punch's attitude to life. As a team, they'd carved up the opposition in horrendous ways.

Right now, Dexter saw in this incessant talking another pointer to the fact that Punch was not being himself.

There was no holding Punch. The patrol had no need to be given exact orders and instructions on what to do, for each man knew his part. So Punch simply passed an acid comment on having to fight carrying all their kit, an eventuality that, whilst not discounted, had not been expected to prove likely. After all, they were supposed to go invisible and keep an obbo.

'If we have to fight the bastards looking like Christmas trees,' and Punch gave his pack a savage shove up on its straps, 'then we'll bloody well do it. Ready?'

Three nods answered him.

Dexter bunged over a couple of HE grenades, and SS followed up with a smoke. The smoke began to spew out off to the left and the wind, still light as yet, drifted it across the front.

Dingle went off first, crouched over. His pack stuck up a mile. Dexter followed, keeping his rifle angled across his body, feeling the weight of all that monstrous equipment straining to push him flat on his face and then, so it seemed, to go on pushing him into the ground.

SS went off next, with Punch bringing up the rear but well up. As he left cover he flung another smoke grenade behind him, the canister landing precisely on the spot he'd earmarked. The fresh gush of smoke lifted up a few feet abaft the first, both adding to the cover and extending it.

A snapping crackle of rifle shots blasted out. The Argies were shooting blind through the smoke at the last position in which they had spotted their enemy – by that time the Brits were long gone.

The low ridge over which they forced themselves at a tremendous pace under smoke cover might be a mere ruffle of ground; once over the crest they would be able to conceal themselves fully from observation from the other side.

The day, such as it was, did not look promising.

The weather was a little on the chilly side; but nothing like what it would be soon. The mist could hardly be said to be burned away by the sun; but there was sunshine and the clumps of vegetation against the barrenness of the peaty ground came as a welcome relief. There was not a single tree on any of the islands of the Falklands, at least, so Dexter had been told. Funny old place, not having any trees. The damned wind, which would get up soon, must be one of the answers, he supposed.

Following Punch, who had taken the lead, Dexter concentrated on the task in hand. The Falklands had a special climate, unique to the islands, and he would have to make use of it whenever he could. A good Strike Force man took everything into account and turned everything to his own advantage.

The bandage on Punch's head would need to be looked at and, not for the first time, Dexter wished he knew a damn sight more about concussion and compressions of the brain. In this inflated mood Punch might do anything.

Pretty soon they'd have to think about holing up. The Argies were unpredictable about how quickly they'd follow up.

If they were a low-morale lot, badly-led, they might hover about for a long time before starting out. If they had a good quality officer to drive them, however, they could limber up and start the pursuit very quickly.

By that time Dexter wanted to be invisible.

Suddenly, Punch called back: 'Ha! We gave 'em the old fish and chip routine back there, Joker!'

Striding on, the CSM staggered. He missed his footing and tumbled down, and all his massive strength couldn't hold him up against the weight of his pack and the kit draped about him.

He fell full length.

Dexter reached him as Punch turned up his face.

'Joker! I can't see! Joker – I'm blind!'

Chapter Four

Jack the Joker Dexter simply said: 'Grab him.'

SS and Dingle each gripped one of Punch's arms and helped him to his feet.

'Joker – I can't see!'

'Take it easy. That's the bang on your head. It'll go ...'

'*Joker!*'

'Get moving!'

Punch, blind though he was, heard and recognized that note in Dexter's voice. Perhaps *because* he was blind, that ugly rasp of command, issued by a man who knew what he was doing and meant, by God Almighty!, to make everyone else do what they were told, reached him even more clearly. Punch Fuller trusted the Joker. He trusted any oppo of Strike Force, of course – that went without saying; but of them all, he fancied he'd put his entire trust in Jack Dexter. He'd already had to when they'd been doing the fish and chip racket ...

Out front Dexter scanned the back trail. The trouble with a lot of this part of the Falklands, he decided, was the absence of decent cover. Oh, sure, any trained man of the major's Strike Force could hide in a crease in the ground and remain undetected, but there were limits. The orange-brown and green vegetation and the chunky petrified formations crusting through the soil here and there did not look promising.

He assured himself no Argies were following. He

could trust SS and Dingle to bring poor old Punch along. By God! If anything really bad happened to the big fellow, he'd feel it himself. That bash on the head, well, it had quite clearly been far worse than Punch had made out.

Feeling a raspy intolerance for anyone who might try to get in his way and stop him, Jack Dexter prowled on. They reached a straggling gaggle of the whitey-greyish rocks at the crest of a peaty ridge. This seemed so obvious a place to hide that he ignored it; he wanted somewhere the Argies wouldn't think of looking.

Dingle called: 'Joker. We've gotta get Punch to –'

'Sure.'

Angrily, Dexter stared about the inhospitable features of this part of West Falkland. What a mess!

He kept looking along the backtrail, his head rotating, feeling jut like the poet put it – like the tail turret of a Lancaster. He wouldn't answer for the consequences if a bunch of those idiot Argies showed up before they'd got Punch safely stowed away.

It just wasn't a part of Strike Force's operational procedures to go prancing about in broad daylight like a bunch of wallies. During the daytime they hid up in their lairs and kept up an obbo, all duly logged in the book. At night they came out and if the need arose they did nasties to the hostiles.

'Joker!' called Dingle again.

'I know, I know.'

Instantly, he castigated himself for those stupid words. Just because Punch was out of it, and they were responsible for him, was that any reason for him to act like a wally himself?

The breeze began to get up. Punch now walked between the two Smiths in what was to Dexter, a frighteningly docile way. The big fellow was acting as though the wrath of God had struck him. His head drooped as he walked, hung down, and then, with a jerk that clearly demonstrated all Punch's willpower, lifted again and the blind eyes stared unseeingly ahead.

They had the next beach to recce. All right, then, he'd damn well go down there now. Dexter made up his mind. Hide in a nice good dry cave overlooking the beach, almost like the one back there. The Argies might very well think that the British would not choose the same bolthole twice.

'This way.'

They headed off towards the shore.

Dexter favoured Punch with a critical look. He decided to gee up the big fellow.

'Hey, Punch, d'you feel as bad as you look?'

Punch reacted.

'I feel fine, 'cept for ...'

'Yeah, but you can't see yourself.'

'Get lost, Joker. Give me a cane and I'll beat you to the target, anytime.'

Slightly more satisfied that the old Punch he knew still clung stubbornly to this shambling blind figure, Dexter concentrated all his attention on the environs of the beach ahead.

One of the maxims instilled into Strike Force by Major Dan Granville was: 'If the hostiles shoot one leg off, hop along on the other. If they shoot that one off, pull yourself along by your fists. If they shoot one arm off, use the other. If they shoot the other one off – use your imagination.'

To the lads this saw became known as the 'Major's Shaft of Imagination'.

From the Falklands back to England is eight thousand miles, and a year or so back in time, Punch Fuller and Jack Dexter, still serenely sober, were trying to chat up a couple of nice girls in the local disco. Flashing lights and heavy music gave conversations a bizarre infrequency, but the girls got the message all right.

'But you're so *big*!' said the one wearing pants which clung to her roundness in a most tantalizing way, the zip appearing ready to burst open at any moment. She laughed in an affected way and nudged her friend, who was thinner and wearing a scent just a trifle too strong for Dexter's taste.

'You have to use your Shaft of Imagination,' said Dexter, and laughed, and Punch threw his head back and laughed, and Ernie Day came over with a beer in his fist and wanted to know the joke.

They told him, whilst the two girls looked on with great suspicion. They figured these characters were from a rugby team, because they looked so – so strong and powerful, so capable of taking knocks.

Not as tall or as obviously robust as Dexter, Ernie Day was a member of the team, an oppo, and a fellow with whom they'd had some good nights out.

Punch said. 'No chance for you here, Ernie – she's spoken for.' He winked at the plump girl. They weren't at name stage just yet.

Her friend giggled and slid her eyes sideways at Dexter.

Ernie took a sip of his beer. 'Can't stay, anyway. Gotta go up and see my folks.'

The way he spoke alerted both Punch and Dexter instantly. You didn't serve alongside a bloke and not get to know a bit about him.

'Trouble?'

'Dunno. Sam, my brother, sounded a bit off on the blower.'

'Well, if you've wangled some compassionate leave whilst we're off to Wales –'

'Nah. Just a quick trip in and out. See what's up. Be back inside forty-eight.'

As Ernie sipped his beer and wandered off, they could

see he was jumpy. He made no attempt to muscle in on one of the girls, as he would normally have done, given their usual friendly rivalry. Punch looked back after him.

'Something's eating our Ern.'

'Yeh. Well, he'll tell us if he wants to.'

Then they went back to the serious business of the evening.

When they packed up to go off to Wales for a spot of physical, Ernie Day hadn't rejoined the unit.

Captain Tom Burnaby didn't make a big fuss about that; anything could have happened and the men of SSF were not the deserting kind. They wouldn't be in Major Dan Granville's mob in the first place, would they?

Captain Guy Wheaton felt they ought to get on to the local police and ask them to check it out, discreetly. Strike Force, in transit to Wales, was not in a position to ring around all the local hospitals.

The Welsh Physical was a mere routine toughener, a trundle through horrors of terrain and obstacles which they'd all done before, to keep them up to standard. Up to snuff, as Guy said, with great satisfaction.

Pain was a phenomenon of the senses, and if you switched it around you could use it as an assist. Some of the lads simply blocked it out. All of them could continue to function with levels of pain flooding their nervous systems that, without their training and dedication, would have finished them instantly.

Guy stormed up with the news as they came in from a hack carrying mammoth burdens, muddy, wet, cold and yet in full command of themselves. Someone had once said, not understanding, that all the men of Special Strike Force looked alike. They were all hard, craggy-featured, firm of lip and jaw, taciturn to strangers, giving nothing away. Yet anyone in the unit knew that every single member of Strike Force was an individual. Each one was unique.

35

'Ernie,' said Captain Guy Wheaton. He looked savage and sick, at the same time. 'Ernie's dead.'

They all waited, grim-faced, poised. Each man of Strike Force was a comrade, each man someone you counted on in times of trouble. The fact that Sergeant Ernie Day was dead affected them all, each and every one.

'The local police rang. Accident. They didn't sound forthcoming, and I don't know all the details.'

'Someone will have to go up for the funeral,' said Tom Burnaby. 'They can find out.'

Punch and Dexter, together, said: 'We'll go.'

Because of the circumstances it was going to be a civilian funeral, and Punch and Dexter went up in civvies. A wreath had been organized from a local florist's. The major considered it proper, civilian funeral or no damn civilian function, that Ernie's red beret should be placed on the coffin. Punch carried it, personally, folded inside his jacket.

No one, not a single soul, made any supposedly funny remarks about them getting out of the Welsh Physical.

They hired a car, a dark blue Granada, and arrived only just in time. The funeral wended its way as funerals do, depressing and yet, with the pertinent remarks of the minister, uplifting in its uncompromising declaration that life and death are real. Dexter didn't enjoy the experience; Punch said not a single solitary word.

The red beret among the flowers, the coffin lowered into the grave.

They went over to speak to Ernie's father and mother. His brother, Sam, a couple of years older and yet gangly and frail beside the toughness of Ernie, wearing spectacles, looked haggard. The sister, Harriet, couldn't stop blubbering, her round face a glisten of red, her handkerchief sodden.

'Perhaps you'd like to come back to the shop, Mr

Fuller?' suggested Mrs Day.

'If that is –' began Dexter, as Punch's lips remained firmly closed. 'Yes. We'd like to – you know – hear about Ernie.'

At the shop in a side turning off the main drag Dexter looked up at the sign. The lines were just wobbly enough and the letters not quite balanced enough to brand the red and yellow signwriting as amateur. He liked it, though, even although he was not enamoured of fish.

DAY'S FISH PARLOUR

Signs fixed in the window above the blue and white checked cloth indicated that whilst fish and chips were the main item, Day's was progressive enough also to serve various pies, chicken and chips and scampi and chips. When Mr Day pushed the door open a bell rang with a clacking, innocent carillon.

As Dexter and Punch had expected, the place was scrupulously clean. The rounded aluminium covers to the fryers gleamed. Glassware shone. The salt and vinegar dispensers were new and spick and span and perfectly free from unpleasant signs around their lips. Mrs Day motioned the small party, which included a few friends, to go into the back parlour. Punch felt like a bull in a china shop – but the sensation was familiar to him and in this context could not unsettle him. Dexter and Punch just found seats and faded into the upholstery.

There ensued a slight argument among the Day family members while deciding whether or not to open that night. It was all low-key, tear-choked, stiff-upper-lip-pish, yet Dexter clearly detected a note of intense strain in Sam.

He did not wish to open; the father and mother did. This alignment puzzled Dexter. Harriet tried to put in a word from time to time and succeeded only in further soaking her procession of handkerchiefs.

The death of a brother was bound to knock a fellow over, yet Dexter, assessing Sam with a casual glance that took in a great deal, saw that Sam was nervous and carried some of the classical symptoms of repressed fear. In short, Sam was more apprehensive than grieving.

The ritual of the cold ham and early salad, the passing out of drinks, all the sentiment attached to this watered-down late twentieth century civilized and respectable descendant of a rip-roaring warrior's send-off to Valhalla passed in time. Eventually, only Dexter and Punch were left, remaining at the Days' invitation to tell them about their son.

They tried to be kind, and Punch unglued his harsh lips to back-up Dexter's words, saying: 'Yes, Mrs Day. Ernie was not just a good soldier, he was a fine bloke. You have every right to be proud of him.'

For Punch, that was bugles, flags and flowers.

And it was damned-well true.

In that moment Dexter felt the reality of the sense of loss Ernie's death had brought, to him and to Punch and the rest of Strike Force. A good mate had bought it in a dumb, stupid accident.

Both men wanted to know about the accident, but the subject had not been brought up, it seemed to them by common consent, and both were puzzled as to the best way of probing without giving offence. Punch simply gave up the struggle, and fancied he'd go around to the local factory in the morning and ask. Dexter felt annoyance surfacing through his feeling of grief for Ernie, annoyance that he couldn't think of a way to ask Ernie's folks this upsetting question.

Punch figured they could simply go around to the local police station and ask; but that seemed a roundabout way of going about it to him. Eventually, when an apposite break occurred in the conversation, he licked his lips and said, 'You didn't tell us about the accident.'

Mrs Day said, 'It was a tragedy, a tragedy.'

Mr Day said nothing.

Sam took off his spectacles and wiggled them about, opened his mouth, said, 'Ah ...' and closed his lips.

'He was a good son.' Mrs Day put a corner of her handkerchief to her eye. Her face looked as though someone had rasped down it with sandpaper. 'A tragedy.'

Harriet stood up. The sodden piece of linen twisted and compressed in her fingers. She was younger than the brothers, around twenty-one or so, judged Dexter, a round-faced, rather plump and, from what Ernie had said, a sweet-natured girl. Her eyes were puffed red and ugly.

She half-turned to face the men from Strike Force.

Sam put his spectacles on quickly.

'Now, Harriet ...'

'It's not fair!' she burst out with a passion that shook her. 'It was not an ...'

'*Harriet!*' Sam's voice broke in violently.

She flinched.

Then she clapped her handkerchief to her face, swung about and, with a chopped-off gabble of inarticulate words, fled from the room.

Chapter Five

The sun was halfway down to the horizon of West Falkland when the first Pucara flew over. The aircraft might only be a light twin-engined job, however, the little terrors packed an almighty punch from cannon, rockets and bombs.

Ensconced in an uncomfortable cleft in the rocks, Dexter stared up through a gap left between the edges of the poncho. The two Smiths kept their heads down, and Punch maintained a steady stream of invective on Argies, Pucaras, blindness, not being able to see, and where's my white cane, Joker?

'Dunno how long it'll last, Punch. But it's got to go away some time, hasn't it?'

'Yeah – when?'

The Pucara circled, with the declining sun catching a long liquid gleam from her wings, and then flew off northwards.

'They've got an airfield up there somewhere,' offered SS to no one in particular.

The thought floated in all their minds.

'Probably on an outlying island,' suggested Dingle.

'We've got to get a Casevac chopper in here for Punch.' Dexter spoke firmly. Although Strike Force operated as a team of individuals, chains of command existed, the major saw to that. With Punch out of it through this cussed blindness, Dexter, as the sergeant, had to assume command. He was prepared to take all kinds of advice from Punch, but he would not accept an order from the tough CSM that would endanger the CSM's chances.

'It'll be dicey flying in —'

'Noggy,' said Dexter, exhibiting perfect confidence in a comrade in Strike Force. 'Noggy'd do it no-handed.'

Lieutenant Noel Oswald Gates, Army Air Corps, had left with the rest of Number One Wing aboard a type 21, and they were off God knew where. Number One Wing included Captain Tom Burnaby, Captain Guy Wheaton and the major himself. Whatever hairy operation they were into was likely to be far more lively than this skulking around carrying on an obbo that, so far, had not gone at all smoothly.

Still, that wasn't absolutely true. As he watched the Pucara vanish away to the north, Dexter had to accept that they'd radioed in reports, checked the beach they were supposed to check, and were about to do the same for this one. No, it was the worry over Punch Fuller that clouded his vision and gave him this jaundiced view of what they'd accomplished so far.

Getting a helicopter in was going to be a pig of a task.

The temperature was still bearable, and the wind, whilst a confounded nuisance, could be lived with. They brewed up and ate, hardly tasting the stuff, and then when the sun finally sank they set off once again.

Punch kept his left arm extended and his fist fastened into the straps of Dexter's jaguar pack. As a result, SS stepped out ahead as point, and Dingle brought up the rear.

The map said there was a charming little bay and a beach that was marked as a possible a few miles up ahead. That was their next objective. Worrying away, Dexter hacked on, feeling the weight on his back and Punch's occasional stumble and subsequent jerk on the pack.

The night remained fine with the high glitter of the stars providing a degree of comfort. Strike Force generally preferred weather that gave them cover for their nocturnal exploits.

The breeze dropped away, as was usual at night, and they moved along soundlessly. Once in a while Punch would put a foot wrong; but he did not open his lips to curse, although he seethed away deep inside that hard shell of his.

What a turn up! What a foul up! Without eyes he felt useless in a way that scared him right down to his socks, a way that no rushing into action and being shot at could remotely equal.

SS stopped dead.

Dexter halted and Punch bumped into him.

Dingle dropped onto one knee to rest the weight of the wireless and pack, his SLR snouting.

Presently, Dexter freed Punch's fist and crawled up to SS. 'Lights.'

Down below they could make out the glimmer of lights on water. They formed a neat rectangle, with one or two outlying beans which were no doubt spots on posts by the wire.

'That's the damned bay we're supposed to recce.'

'Yeah. And the Argies are there.'

'Bit of a camp they've got.'

In the dim glow of a Betalight Dexter checked the map once again. This third possible landing site lay up to the north of the other two. Further north still lay more beaches that were being recced by Sergeant Paul Frost and his patrol, who were, in turn, working their way south. The plan called for the two patrols to meet up – with all due care – and then be lifted out, either by boat or chopper as the occasion warranted. Paul Frost – once known as Ice, then Icey, and now, by a process of elimination, generally called Ickey – was a bloke who didn't take kindly to fumblers.

If the Argies were massed in strength here, the rendezvous would have to be changed.

Just on a long shot, Dexter flipped out his little pocket Scimitar wireless and called out, 'Ickey. Come in, Ickey.'

Nothing hummed back in reply over the air waves.

'If Ickey's on time he ought to be in range pretty soon,' grumbled Punch. 'He's hell on wheels to anyone late on parade.'

The Punch Fuller that Dexter knew and worked with and trusted would never have felt the need to say anything at that point. This new and strange Punch Fuller was a damned unsettling oppo.

'A camp, is it?' said Punch. He was not exactly rambling; but his words were slurred and he stopped and started when he spoke. 'If I c'd see where I was going I'd be down there faster'n a ferret down a rabbit hole.'

'We ain't recced it yet, Punch,' protested SS.

'Only bleeding Argies, ain't they?'

Dexter was impelled to say: 'The Argies are tough little bastards, if they're well led, we all know that.'

'Bunch of flaming conscripts.'

Dingle chipped in: 'Could be their Special Forces –'

'So what?'

Dexter didn't believe this. Here they were, four members of a crack force, jabbering away like a bunch of schoolkids over a visiting eleven. It was just nonsensical.

Then, to cap it all, Punch growled out: 'If the major was here we'd soon be in there, mark my words.'

Jack Dexter realized he had to get a grip on the situation at once. Much more and they'd be drawing up a book on the odds.

'The Argies are equipped more or less like we are. We do this right. We recce the campo and suss it out. We contact Ickey. Then, if the chances are right, we'll go in. Otherwise we leave the buggers strictly alone, as per

43

orders, and signal out to HQ for a lift out.'

He stared at Punch's sightless eyes.

'Anything to add on that, Punch?'

'Not while I can't see a damn thing!'

Still not happy about the whole stupid situation, Dexter sorted out who did what as they settled down.

The three others mucked in to scrape up a hide for Punch and they got the big man down comfortably and ensured he was well-camouflaged. He'd given up pawing at his face and eyes and, every now and then, his big-knuckled hands would grip up into fists and he'd simulate striking out at invisible terrors. He was, Dexter saw, in a bad way and likely to get worse if he didn't get his sight back soon.

Bending over to give the poncho a last finicky adjustment, Dexter felt Punch's enormous hand close around his throat. Instinctively he started to strike out in such a way as to break the grip; then he checked the blow.

Punch's face was contorted. He pawed the camouflage away, rearing up, gripping onto Dexter's neck.

'I've got 'im! I've got the bastard!'

Dexter gargled, trying to speak, and then twisting his fingers around the hand at his throat and heaving.

It was like trying to break a bar of steel across your knee.

The two men thrashed about, with Dexter trying to free himself from that deadly clasp, and the CSM grinding down with every intent of choking the life out of this comrade he saw as an enemy.

Dingle joined in, trying to unwrap Punch's fingers one by one, until a roundhouse blow knocked him headlong across the peaty ground. Dexter's eyes shot black and red sparks. The top of his head felt as though it was going to come off and his lungs were beginning to shriek for air.

SS leaned over and tapped Punch alongside the ear. He

used the handle of his bayonet, the hilt rapping into Punch's skull with exquisite care.

Punch collapsed.

Dexter got that enormous gripping hand away and gulped in air, shaking his head gingerly, feeling his throat. He felt sure his Adam's Apple was crushed to Adam's Cider.

'You two all right?' SS asked, then added, 'pair of bloody wallies. Poor old Punch ...'

Dexter recognized his own faults. He should have broken the grip with a break-lock he knew from *keninja*, the particularly rough and nasty form of martial arts taught in Strike Force. But he had hesitated. And then it would probably have been too late. So much for the dreaded killing reaction, so much for friendship.

Dingle crawled back, swearing, and holding his face.

The damp scent of the night gusted in about them, the smell of the sea, the rawness of the air. A mist began to damp down the sharpness of that rectangle of lights below. And the four man patrol of Strike Force realized the straits they were in, for Punch said: 'Joker? What ...?'

'Nothing, Punch. Get some rest.'

SS whistled.

'Strewth! He must have a head like a cannonball's grown-up brother! I hit him just hard enough to sleepy-bye him — and here he is alive and talking —'

'Effects of a second blow,' said Dingle.

Dexter wondered what Punch was making of all this when the father and mother of all snores rattled and reverberated up. Punch lay flat, mouth wide open, emitting sounds like a herd of pigs on their way over the cliff.

'The disgusting —'

'That's only snoring,' said Dingle. 'Heave him over on his side. He'll be all right 'til morning.'

This time when the big fellow was arranged comfortably he stayed peacefully asleep.

Dingle went on watch. SS wanted to brew up, and Dexter was detailed to catch up on his sleep. They'd rotate the watch and the rest. They had all night and all tomorrow before working out their next move.

Crawling into his sleeping bag, Dexter could still feel that frightful pressure around his neck. By God! Old Punch could have throttled him!

And known nothing about it, God help him.

His eyes closed. That snoring – Patsy had a snore on her that could slam the windows shut across the room.

Every time he nudged her and tried to heave her over into a new position she'd wake up, sleepily, and then come wide awake fully anticipating him being ready and after another session. She wasn't sure if she should believe she snored or not; but as they were both awake and it was damned hot in the hotel and the bed was comfortable, they might as well make the most of these opportunities.

They'd used good old Thomas Cook Esquire to arrange their holiday, and had chosen Fuengirola, between Torremolinos and Marbella on the Costa del Sol.

'We'll go there, Jack,' said Patsy, 'because I've never heard of it, and all the girls in the office know Marbella and Torremolinos.'

'If you say so.'

It turned out fine. Patsy lolled about with a bikini that resembled a piece of toffee paper on a string and a couple of postage stamps on another piece of string. She tanned beautifully. Dexter was already hard-tanned, more from wind than sun.

She had a way with her, had young Patsy, of pushing her heavy dark hair back and looking up and under at you that did unconscionable things to Jack Dexter's spine. She liked a good romp, too, which was important. But, she did chatter. She talked about the girls in the office, and various pop groups and their latest hit singles and what albums they were releasing, and what were the chances of her getting to see her favourites on their tours. Her taste in music was not shared by Dexter. She talked about her family, in a most patronizing way, and particularly of her sister, whom she professed to detest beyond all detestations on Earth.

They had met — almost inevitably given the separate nature of their normal lives — at a disco. Still, she was a good kid and liked pretty things. She'd insisted on helping to pay for the Costa del Sol holiday with Thomas Cook, and Dexter had given in to her somewhat fierce protests. She liked to swing free, as she put it.

When he contemplated what he'd do if she went off with another fellow — and there were plenty of sun-tanned beach boys about — he realized with some amusement that he'd feel a touch of sorrow at lost opportunities; but that would be all. She was nice, yes; yet there were always plenty more.

Next time he'd hope to find a nice girl who didn't have a snore on her that could flutter the curtains out horizontal.

The bizarre contrast of the sun-drenched Spanish beaches and the bleak terrain around him now in the Falklands afforded plenty of food for thought. Oh, sure, he knew why he was down here. The Argies had used naked force to grab what was not theirs, despite their erroneous beliefs, and if they were allowed to get away with it, all hell might break loose.

Who knew who might next decide that a few isolated Brits living somewhere over the sea from Britain were easy prey?

Dexter mumbled around with his tongue, trying to get rid of what felt like a furry overcoat, then Dingle and SS

47

came in and he went out on watch. A few clouds overhead obscuring the stars brought visibility right down. He used the nightscope and checked over the camp, before deciding that nothing much was doing there. The Argies were all tucked up comfortably in their little beds – they'd have tents for sure and possibly pre-fab huts if their logistics people had got it right. They were laughing now, all right.

He made sure Punch was still sleeping peacefully and then resumed his vigil.

Fifteen minutes later he was astonished to see a black form emerge from Punch's lair. He twisted his head around to watch. The CSM stood up, then dropped to a crouch and started off for Dexter. In those few moments he'd spotted the layout, seen the others in their hides, noted the obvious place for the sentry and was now taking himself off there to find out what was going on.

Dexter said: 'What the hell are you doing, Punch? You're supposed to –'

'I can see, Joker!'

'I realize that –'

'It takes more than a little knock on the head to put Punch Fuller out of it, boyo!'

They spoke in short breathy gusts; no one more than a few yards away would have heard a thing.

'You're still not fit –'

'Cobblers! What's going on?'

Dexter roughed-out what had happened.

At his side Punch shifted his night glasses forward and took a look towards the camp and the sea.

'Now that is nice,' he said in a reflective voice. 'That is very interesting.'

Instantly, Dexter slapped up his own night sight and took a squint. A dim shape was slipping in from the sea towards the bay. They could hear no heavy beat of engines, but they both knew what they were looking at.

48

'They're running in a ship through the Exclusion Zone, boyo!'

'Yeh. There's a couple to three hours to daylight yet. They've timed it pretty neatly.'

'I wonder what they've got aboard. Ammo? Supplies? Men?'

'Why here?'

Punch's massive frame stirred and he let out a soft, gusty sigh.

'I'm not wondering any more, Joker.'

'No,' said Dexter, resigned. 'I guessed not.'

'Rouse out SS and Dingle. We're going to take a little mosey down there and suss out what's what. And if we do fit in a little spot of malletting as well — won't that be fun?'

Chapter Six

Major Dan Granville, when he'd been bashing the men he'd selected for his Special Strike Force into shape, often used to say: 'You're hunters. So think like hunters. When you do a stalk select the objective and go for it, hit it, and don't take no for an answer.'

Anybody who did not measure up to Granville's stringent and almost superhuman demands was RTU. Returned To Unit was the polite way of saying they were Chucked Out. If you got a CO from Granville, he'd always come around and tell you. Unlike other outfits. Granville wanted the best, selected all his people personally and usually got first choice, one notable exception being Captain Tom Burnaby who ran the Signals side. When WOII Arthur Fuller led Sergeant Jack Dexter with Lance Corporals Sidney and Alf Smith down onto the camp, to mosey around and see what they could find out and perhaps mallet anything that got in the way, they knew exactly what they were doing.

They wouldn't have been in Strike Force otherwise.

So that meant there was no need for orders apart from directives as to objectives, no need to talk, no need to raise the spirits. When Strike Force struck – they struck!

Like savage hunters of the jungle, then, they advanced on the objective – but they were not savage animals, they were not wild barbarians, they were trained soldiers, professionals, rational thinking men highly tuned to a pitch that enabled them to perform actions other men might not credit. They were not savages. They were not murdering cannibals; they were professional fighting men carrying out the tasks for which they had been superbly trained.

Just before they came up with the first of the tents they crossed an expanse of flat ground where the going was much firmer. Not one of the four needed either to tell or be told: they all knew they were walking over a helicopter landing area.

That was one for the log.

They had absolutely no difficulty in getting in among the huts and tents. They saw no sentries on this southern face, and guessed all the interest and labour in the camp would be concentrated on the approaching vessel.

Each man was stripped down to fighting kit. Dexter felt reasonable confidence that no one would stumble over their cache of equipment. He'd seen no sense in trying to dissuade Punch from this escapade. He knew the big fellow! Right or wrong, they were committed, and he'd loyally follow his comrades into action.

At that, they ought to do some good here, further the cause, and then high-tail it out before the Argies realized what had hit them.

The patrol was not in the business of killing Argentinians. They would like to cause a great deal of mischief, cause the Argies as much unpleasantness as they could. The Argies had come pushing in where they were not wanted. The old song said the grass is greener in Argentina – that was probably a bit of propaganda, anyway – so the stupid damned Argies could sod off back home.

Everything was communicated in sign language, either at the distance they could see in the darkness or by hand pressure. They were carrying a fair old supply of plastic explosives and the four men of Strike Force immediately

51

went off hungrily, looking for places where they could bung the plastic to good effect.

They found a wooden hut bolted together in an irregular square-shape which looked promising, so they fixed the plastic, set the little timer and moved off. They were in no hurry, yet they moved like water on a greased frying pan. Two more huts were fitted up. Dexter moved on ahead and saw ahead the tell-tale roseate flicker of a cigarette end between two tents.

If the stupid bastards had to smoke cigarettes that was A Okay by him. One way or another, they'd get themselves killed if they weren't careful.

Punch put his ferocious fingers around Dexter's hand and squeezed out: 'They're mine!'

Dexter let him go.

Presently the cigarette ends plopped onto the ground. Dexter moved up.

Opening those harsh lips that had so recently been opened most uncharacteristically loquaciously, Punch whispered, 'I wanta have a dekko at that ship.'

Dingle said, 'We didn't bring the LAWs.'

'A bit of plastic fixed to the waterline, boyo. That'll bring tears to their eyes.'

Dexter said, 'I'll go.'

The others didn't argue. They knew Dexter was the best swimmer and underwater man in the patrol.

And, of course, this was where this kind of leadership – from the front, baldheaded – worried Dexter. They'd not properly recced the camp or the beach and bay. They knew nothing of the ship. Nevertheless, whilst the thing was there it was his duty to try to sink the ship. Nothing else would be tolerated in Strike Force, least of all by the Joker Dexter. The patrol moved warily off towards the sea line.

They had to circle to avoid the huts and tents ahead. It was not difficult to guess that the Argies were busily unloading the vessel right now. They were using lights, although these were subdued. Punch led off to the side and soon they were standing on the near-side edge of the bay with the beach spread out before them. The dark mass of the ship bulked against the sheen of the water. Muffled noises reached them; the sound of boots, the clank of iron chains, the occasional shrill yell as an officer exhorted his men to get the lead out. Sounds carried. As Dexter saw it, stripping off everything which was not essential, even if the Argies did land this cargo, the ship would never make another run through the Exclusion Zone once he'd finished with it.

Punch's usually confident voice sounded odd. Over the period since he'd suffered that knock on the head he'd been overconfident, brash. Now he sounded dubious.

'Joker? It's damned cold.'

'Won't be in long enough.'

'Make sure you're not. You won't have long, anyway. Joker −'

'I know, Punch.'

Dingle, in his medic's voice, said: 'I'd better go as back up −'

'No!' answered Punch and Dexter together.

There was no need for histrionics. Dexter settled himself, made sure his knife was in its sheath, that the plastic in its wrappings was lashed to his waist, and waded in.

Good Gordon Bennet!

The cold bit him everywhere with steel fangs and he could feel his body heat leaching away. The lash of that cold made him feel he was having his skin flayed off. Resolutely, he plunged in and struck out for the hull of the ship. They'd tracked in as far as they could along the beach, probably too far for complete safety, and there wasn't a long way to go. He knew he could do it. If he'd thought that the task was beyond his competence he wouldn't have gone in the first place.

You didn't get into Strike Force by playing silly buggers. He made no noise through the water. Each breath of air either resembled swallowing an icicle or a red-hot poker, he couldn't decide. His body was just a mechanism which needed to be made to perform certain tasks. He swam on.

The side of the ship, black as midnight, reared up over his head. The plates were harsh with rust under his fingers. He had to do this thing right, do it the first time, do it quick – and get the hell out of it.

The plastic clapped onto the rusty hull all right and the timer went in. The cold about him now seemed to have gone away and he felt as if he was floating in a milk bath. So that was it, then.

He would never have the time to swim back to where the lads waited for him now, for the cold was far more intense than he'd expected. Inured as he was to pain and privation, the insidiousness of this attack would come in its very absence of sensations. He snapped on the timer, pushed off from that rusty old hull and began to swim.

He did not head back the way he had come. He had to make a decision, and being the Joker he had taken some pleasure from the speed with which he'd reached that decision. It was, after all, a joke – a joke on him …

Dexter swam directly for the beach following shortest possible line. He knew in a matter of only moments he'd be done for.

Training, toughness, professionalism, the knowledge that he was a member of the elite Strike Force, carried Dexter through. He and Punch hadn't realized just what was involved when he'd started off. He'd bitten off more than any normal human being could be expected to chew; but he'd damn well chew it, all of it, and spit out the pips, as Punch Fuller would say. He'd damn well do so ...

Sensation no longer existed. His arms struck and drew back, struck and drew back, his legs kicked and kicked. He was a mere machine, a machine of flesh and blood performing a task to tax a machine of steel and iron. He swam. Oh, yes, Jack the Joker Dexter swam, he swam for his life.

The only thing that mattered was to reach the shore.

Once he'd done that – once – he could start to think about something other than this continuous slogging progress through the water. The water felt like syrup, like lead. It bound his arms and legs. His chest hurt. He breathed and it was as though fire and ice entered deeply into his body.

The beach swished up and hit him in the chest and a wave carried him further on – and still he continued those reflex swimming actions, driving on. Water drained away past his prone body and he realized he was on land. The shingle shifted and slid about him. The smell of wetness clung. With an effort which originated in the deepest recesses of his mind he got a knee under himself, pushed, staggered up to his feet, reeling.

Blearily, he stared around.

His strength was being sapped away now with frightening speed. He had to get under cover and get dry or – well, there was no or about it. He had to.

A flashlight beam scythed abruptly across the beach from the darkness. It swung away to his right and instantly he turned to his left. He took three heavy strides across the shingle, feeling as though he was climbing Mount Everest in his pyjamas carrying concrete blocks attached everywhere to his body. A buzzing in his head and ears sounded like lumber being sawn into planks for coffins.

The light switched back, travelled along the beach. He threw himself flat and the light settled, pooled about him, pinned him. Voices shouted.

Heavy boots about him, excited voices gabbling, hands grabbing him and lifting ...

When Jack Dexter more or less came back to the world and reality he was lying on a pile of sacks in a hut, more sacks thrown over him, shivering as though he had a fever, and feeling as though he'd been dumped into a concrete mixer for half-a-day's pay.

A swarthy-faced man with plump cheeks leaned over him.

'You will live, Englishman.'

Instantly, Dexter was in control of himself.

He couldn't see his wristwatch and he most certainly wasn't going to look now. He'd no idea of how much time had elapsed. Had the explosions gone off – or were they to come?

He said: 'What happened?'

It was vitally necessary to give nothing away.

'I was going to ask you that.'

The man's English was very good, marred only by the accent. This was to be expected. The hut smelt oddly, of oil and sardines and tar. He couldn't see much of it as yet. He let out a groan and did not have to contribute much faking to make it sound genuine.

'You are in pain?'

'Bloody cold –'

'Yes. Why were you in the water?'

'Fell in, didn't I? Thought I was a gonner.'

'A – gonner? Ah, yes. You did not believe you had survival value.'

'You can say that again. Thanks for pulling me out.'

Let 'em sort that gambit out.

'From where did you fall?'

Dexter liked that grammatical construction.

'Off the damn edge. Foot gave. Thought it was all over for me.'

'Yes. The edge? The edge of what?'

'Ground here's rotten, anyway. Don't trust it.'

With a rustle that echoed in the little hut the Argentine unfolded a map and spread it on the sacks. Dexter shoved himself up into a half-sitting position. Well, he knew what the Falklands looked like.

'Perhaps you would be good enough to point out to me where you fell off the edge?'

Now Dexter began to sift through various ideas on all this. The man hadn't asked his name, rank and number so Dexter was still, apparently, in the grip of his ghastly ordeal. Well, he damned well was, wasn't he? There had been no offer of creature comforts, no cigarette, no spirits, no hot drink. This fellow was a bit of a psychologist, then. He was in on the inside curve, hoping to catch the English soldier with all his defences down.

Quite clearly, this Argie had never heard Major Dan Granville stating one of his maxims: 'You'll never catch my lads with their pants down, even in the lavatory.'

He looked at the map, spotted the bay and beach, selected the one they'd left earlier and waved his forefinger over the map as though undecided. Then he stabbed it down.

'Right here. I think.'

'You were lost?'

Dexter seized the chance as though he stood in the slips and the ball had snicked the bat's shoulder.

'Well – yes, I was.'

The only light in the hut from the paraffin lamp, which contributed more than its quota of smells to the atmosphere, shaded the man's face. Dexter's own pugnacious features were composed and, he hoped, a trifle fuddled-looking. The fellow wore a camouflage outfit and looked real natty.

'Would you like to know the time, Englishman?'

'Don't make much difference now, does it?'

Dexter – any fellow of Strike Force – wasn't to be caught by a chestnut like that.

Clear indecision marked that plump and swarthy face. This had been the kid-gloves, psychological section. Dexter wondered how much longer he had – and then a thought hit him, a thought that, whilst it was horrific, was so much in keeping with his nickname that he had the devil of a job from busting out laughing.

What a joke! On the Joker!

He was in this damned hut and in all probability a chunk of plastic was gently timing itself to blow the lot to kingdom come. And if the joke was planned correctly that bang would go off just by his right ear, next to the hut wall. What, as Andy would say, a monumental cock-up!

Chapter Seven

After they left Day's Fish Parlour, Punch and Dexter put up at a small hotel and, early the next morning, they went around to the local police station. As Dexter said, 'Let's get all this sorted out sharpish.'

Punch, with his usual closed-lips manner, said nothing. His face revealed a great deal, however, and Dexter was well aware they both shared a sense of puzzlement. Harriet's outburst had been passed over, no more was said one way or the other by Sam or his parents. Dexter was assailed by nasty feeling that this whole business was nowhere near being settled.

The desk sergeant proved to be gruffly polite and he passed them over to a young DC whose eyes already betrayed a man wise in the ways of villainy in the world. He remembered the case clearly enough, and confirmed it was an accident. What he told Punch and Dexter made them feel savage.

'His face?'

'Yes,' said Detective Constable Marshall. 'His brother found him. He'd evidently slipped and fallen against the fish fryers. Banged his head. Knocked himself out. Fell face-down into the boiling oil.'

Neither of the men from Strike Force said anything for a time after that. The picture was too hideous, even for hardened cases like themselves.

After a bit Dexter asked, 'How come you were involved?'

'The sister called us in. She was incoherent, as you'd expect. When she calmed down there was nothing to it, so I just filed the report.'

'How d'you mean, nothing to it?'

'Well, you know how these things get blown up. She thought it might not have been an accident at first. But it clearly was – no sign of foul play, open and shut.' The DC spoke like this to civilians for a variety of reasons, one of which was to polish the 'image' the super kept on about.

There was precious little more they could learn, and after a few more words, they cleared off. It wasn't opening time yet. Dexter started off firmly for the pair of red telephone boxes on the corner. Punch ambled along after him.

The number of the fish shop was easily found in the phone book and Dexter dialled out.

'Mrs Day? This is Jack Dexter – look, I'm sorry to bother you. Could I have a word with Sam, please?'

'He's not in – no, he's gone out. Had to see some friends – I'm sorry –'

'Not to worry. Any idea when he'll be back?'

'No, not really …'

'Well, thank you, anyway.'

He put the phone down very very carefully, when he felt like smashing it back into its cradle.

'Look, Punch, there's something fishy about this – and I ain't making no jokes.'

'Yeh. So what d'we do?'

'You going to get on to Barky, or me?'

'You.'

'Thought so.'

Barky was Lieutenant Miles Barker, who was running Number Three Wing at the time. He'd report in to the major and spread the word. No member of SSF was going to like *that*.

60

When he'd finished the bald report of the facts over the phone to Lieutenant Miles Barker, Dexter added: 'I'd like to hang on for another day, if that's all right. I want to speak to Ernie's sister. I've got a nasty feeling everything's not kosher up here.'

Barky made up his mind instantly.

'Right. I'll square it with the major. I just hope you're wrong, Joker.'

'Me too.'

He let the phone booth door swing shut and turned to Punch, who was leaning up against the other booth staring moodily at the traffic and the passers-by, trying to find an attractive pair of legs to gawp at and having no luck.

'Right, Punch, it's on. But we ought to tackle the girl gently. Harriet. Make it kind of casual.'

'Yeh. You're right.'

There were ways and ways of asking questions. The men of Strike Force, like the other Special Forces, were trained in resisting. It was all highly unpleasant and no one wanted to find themselves in the position where the training would have to be put to use. As for asking questions themselves, they were handy at that, too ...

Sitting on a pile of smelly sacks and feeling as though he'd been run over by a traction-engine, Jack Dexter's mind drifted back to his present situation as he wondered if he should use his training right away or wait until he'd been blown to Kingdom Come by his own explosives.

What a foul up! Yet whatever happened to him could only be a small part of the total that made up this business of removing the Falklands from the hot and sticky grasp of the thieving Argies.

The plump-faced Argentine captain pulled out a fancy silver cigarette case, flipped it open and proferred it to Dexter. Dexter shook his head. The captain looked surprised, lit up himself with as fancy a lighter, spewed

61

out a stinking cloud of foul cigarette smoke into the hut and sat back on the chair he'd hooked up with a heel.

So now comes part two of the session, said Dexter to himself.

On a gust of dank and chilly wind the door opened and a soldier humped through. He did not look anywhere near as happy or as contented with his lot as the captain.

A quick gabble of Spanish, the soldier dumped down his bundle, and then the captain made an unmistakable rude gesture for the man to clear off. He went out and slammed the door. The hut and the door looked solid, old and clapped out, and Dexter guessed this was probably a kelper's hut used for fishing tackle or some such, not one of the prefab jobs brought over in the invasion.

'Here are your clothes, Englishman. We have dried them for you.'

Dexter felt he wouldn't be breaking the Geneva convention if he said 'Thank you'. At the same time he remembered someone telling him the Argies had never signed the said convention. He put on his clothes. There were no boots or socks. The captain smiled and puffed smoke.

'So you fell off the cliff, in only these clothes, no anorak, and no shoes and socks? Really!'

'Managed to get out of them in the water.'

'As you would say – pigs can fly.'

Dexter remained as silent as Punch.

The captain leaned forward and disgusting cigarette smoke wafted into Dexter's face. He remained unmoving; but he could not prevent his lips from curling in distaste.

'Let me tell you the truth, Englishman. Then you will give me your name and the rest of the information. You belong to the Special Attack Group. Why not admit it? You are here to sabotage our installations.'

Amusement, incongruously enough, hit Dexter then. The Special Attack Group was run by Colonel Armstrong, generally known to his friends as Zit, although no one knew why, and he was as rough, tough and maniacal as Major Dan Granville.

Strike Force and the Attack Group had had a go at each other up in the wilds of Northern Canada, and the fact that no one had been killed was a sheer miracle. That was the time Tom Burnaby and Pugsy had pinched a sno-cat from under the Special Attack Group's red noses. Still, the two outfits co-operated well when they had to, even if each sought ways and means – usually evil means – of stealing a march on the other. And anything else that wasn't nailed down.

He shook his head and reached for the dry clothes.

'I do not belong to them, haven't heard of 'em.'

In putting on his clothes he sneaked a look at his wristwatch. He was not naive enough to feel disappointment, or anger, just resignation. Another monumental cock-up, then …

His head down, he took a good hard look at the captain's boots. The scrutiny revealed they were smart but effective footwear, like the Argie boots, and their size would just about do. Give him a minute or two to get his breath back, and he'd think about a swift visit to the local shoe shop.

'You admit you are a Special Services man, then?'

Dexter did not reply: 'You great wally! Anybody'd know I was Special Forces merely because I'm here!' He just looked up with a hangdog expression and said: 'I admit nothing.'

'You are doing yourself no good.'

The phrase jolted Dexter's memory back into the past. In effect that was precisely what Ernie Day's brother Sam had said when they caught up with him in the local. He was just as jumpy, and he wouldn't look them in the

63

eye. Mind you, anybody with a guilty conscience would find it extraordinarily hard to look Punch Fuller in the eye.

'I told you, Mr Dexter. Harriet was in a state. She didn't know what she was saying.' Sam sank half his pint, taking his time. The pub was sparsely occupied this soon after opening time, and the three men sat on a bench in a window corner away from the bar. Sam lowered his glass. 'I explained all that to the police.'

'Wonder why she should say it wasn't an accident, though,' said Dexter. 'I mean – well, if it wasn't an accident –'

'But it *was*!'

Three men entered the pub and walked over to the bar with just a hint of swagger in their gait. They were smartly dressed in a flashy way, and the middle-sized one even wore two-tone shoes. The big one was on a level with Punch, and looked like a pug, his nose broken, and a flat and almost imbecilic stare in his pale eyes. They ordered and the barman treated them as he would regulars. Dexter watched all this only because of Sam's instant reaction.

Ernie's brother didn't bother to finish the rest of his pint. He stood up and his hand gripped onto the back of the bench. He licked his lips.

'Must get back to the shop. Start peeling.'

Punch looked at Dexter and started to open his mouth. Dexter, feeling regret at having to cut off any of Punch's few and therefore precious words, cut in to say, 'All right, Sam. We might be along later. Have a fish supper. Look forward to it.'

Sam was not deceived. He bent, suddenly, and his thin face flushed up.

'You leave Harriet alone! You hear? Keep her out of it –'

'Out of what?'

Sam swung about and his jacket caught his glass and sent it skating across the marble tabletop. Punch put out a massive hand and caught the glass, cradled it, staring after Sam as he rushed out of the doors like a cyclone.

'Something's itching him, Joker.'

'If it's what I think it is, I feel sorry for him and for Harriet. We'll have to see her, Punch. No other way.'

'Yeh.'

Both soldiers stared speculatively although surreptitiously at the three men at the bar ...

In the fish-smelling hut on West Falkland, Jack Dexter stared speculatively and surreptitiously at the Argie captain's boots. He'd get nowhere without footwear. And a decent anorak. And some grub. And a bondouk if he could lay hands on something decent, with ammo.

The door opened and a young lieutenant came in on the expected gush of cold, dank air. He was a most handsome lad, and he let his liquid stare rest unguardedly on this ferocious British captive. He was followed by a bulky figure in an enormous padded anorak with the hood pulled right up and drawn tight. The door slammed.

The captain stood up quickly.

At once Dexter sensed more trouble. The captain wasn't standing up for the young lieutenant, no matter what they got up to off duty. That meant the figure in the anorak was important. Then he saw what the lieutenant was carrying.

Well, he'd known, of course. But it was hard to take now that the actuality was being rubbed under his nose.

The gabble of Spanish was difficult to follow, and he missed most of it, but he sorted out that everything was now safe. The captain indicated he'd had no luck, and the important personage remarked that now he was here all that would change.

In fluent if slightly accented English, the anoraked figure said, 'You see, Englishman, your plot has failed.'

Dexter said nothing.

The lieutenant carried a mishapen lump of plastic. Dexter couldn't tell which particular piece of the explosive it might be; but he knew that the Argies had been around looking, and had found the charges before they'd exploded.

After a moment of silence that was probably tense for the Argies and certainly miserable for the Briton, the important personage unlatched his hood and threw it back. He looked the sort of man who might enjoy his work. His eyes were clear, his heavily-moustached face regular and even handsome. He was a commanding figure. But there clung to him – and Dexter picked up the vibes plainly enough – the sense of leashed power. He moved forward slowly, drawing off his gloves. In those movements Dexter clearly saw the careful stalk towards the quarry and the unsheathing of the claws.

He opened the front of the anorak and Dexter, expecting to see a flash Argie uniform, was surprised to glimpse a blue blazer and grey slacks.

'I am Captain Hector Caldeiro, the intelligence officer here.'

Calmly, recognizing the new and chilling factor which had entered the situation, Dexter said, 'Then you must recognize I can give you only my name, rank and number.'

'You are at liberty to believe that, if you wish.'

The lieutenant holding the explosive coughed with a gentle sound, and Caldeiro waved him away. He went most thankfully. Dexter did not miss the tension in the young lieutenant and, guessing its origins, again felt that miasmic chill. Well, if he was in for it, he was in for it. All his training, added to his own stamina and willpower, would have to work. Would *have* to work.

Captain Hector Caldeiro took another step forward.

'I wish to know how many of you there are here, where you are, your base. I wish to know everything. And you will tell me, Englishman.'

His fist whipped around in a blur of speed and smashed against Dexter's face.

Chapter Eight

Punch Fuller gripped onto his Sterling Patchett Silenced Gun with both fists. His fingers caught hold with tremendous force. He said nothing, temporarily shedding the new and frightening loquaciousness that had afflicted him since the rifle butt's blow to his head.

The two Smiths crouched by a tumble of rocks along the beach, saying nothing, feeling a great deal. Every man of Strike Force was a comrade, in a very real sense a brother. The loss of anyone struck home cruelly. Yet their comradeship was not simple mawkish friendship. In almost every war and in almost every army, the sage advice was never to make a friend.

If you palled up with a chap and became good friends, if he was killed you felt it worse and could lose your own cutting edge. You might do damn foolish things in moments of crisis instead of doing the right thing.

Punch trusted every member of SSF as a fellow professional. They wouldn't have passed the major's stringent test otherwise. Nevertheless, that didn't mean he had to love each one as a brother.

Some of the turdheads in whom he reposed perfect confidence with his life, in moments of action, were the same men he wouldn't trust with a dud sixpence in the pub while they were both chasing the same girl.

But old Joker, now ... This was cruel. This was damn hard.

The black and featureless expanse of water breathed an evil menace. The scattered lights of the Argie camp remained constant against the blackness where clouds brought the starglitter into a vague and nebulous nothingness, and the smell of the sea wafted up strong and pungent.

'Long past time, Punch,' said Dingle.

'The buggers have found 'em,' said SS. 'And the ship –'

'My fault,' said Punch Fuller. 'My stupid fault. We should have cut shorter fuses and never let Joker go –'

'He could still be alive, Punch, and been captured.'

'If he has the Argies will be sorry.'

Dingle raked the big Scimitar set around and looked up in the darkness at Punch's massive silhouette against that vague nebulous shine in the sky.

'Call out HQ, I reckon, and tell 'em.'

'No. First thing, call out for Ickey.'

'Check.'

Dingle did the honours with his pocket Scimitar. The little radio set, spewing out its signals wobbling up and down the frequencies, would never be intercepted by the Argentines in a month of Sundays. He called out and then everyone felt the boost to their spirits as Paul Frost's voice rode in over the airwaves.

'Ickey here. Punch?'

Dingle replied, 'Yeh. Locate.'

Despite the use of the nicknames that carried their own inbuilt security system, the necessary codes were used on both sides to ensure that no clever-dick Argie had captured a pocket Scimitar and was speaking colloquial English. When Punch and Ickey were satisfied, a rendezvous was arranged. The two patrols would meet up in under two hours. By that time daylight ought to be here and so they took particular care over the rendezvous point.

When he'd done that, Punch told Dingle to call HQ.

His report proved to be succint and brutal.

The response was no less abrasive.

No helicopters were available and the two patrols must vanish themselves on West Falkland until they could be retrieved. No choppers meant no ships available to carry them in, and that meant no Geminis or Rigid Raiders would be available for the patrols to sail out.

Argentine Air Force raids were probing the outlying pickets of the Task Force, and more opposition was expected with each dawn.

When HQ wanted to know the progress of Punch's head injury, he replied in a reflection of his old laconic ways, 'No problem. Just a bump on the noggin.'

Knowing Punch HQ accepted his statement, although Punch himself detected a note of critical concern in Shrimp's words over the air, and therefore repeated: 'Nothing. Just a bump.'

'We'll get the chopper to you soonest. Meanwhile, hang on.'

Cutting the connection, Punch Fuller said in a gruesome attempt at Joker's wit, 'Or get hanged.'

No one paid any attention. Now it was a question of taking the essential items from the four sets of kit, and yomping hard over the terrain to meet up with Ickey. Punch took Joker's Enfield Individual Weapon and ammo, as well as his own Sterling. Most of Dexter's kit had to be left behind; but Punch burdened himself, overburdened himself, with extra LAWs and rations.

At least they were a few pounds light in plastic explosive. And a fat lot of good that had been. A wasted effort and the loss of a comrade – Punch refused to think about that. He'd meet up with Ickey and his patrol and then they'd decide what to do. Their options seemed precious few to him.

SS said: 'We ain't gonna make it by daylight.'

70

'What,' added Dingle, 'they call daylight around here.'

Seeing this was so, Punch had no option but to call out to Ickey again and re-arranged the schedule. He saw this as just another part of all the foul-ups that had plagued this particular recce patrol.

The buzzing persisted in his head, his ears seeming to be vibrating; but that was just a result of that turdhead Argie's rifle butt. The discomfort would go by morning. The bleeding had stopped and he could discard Dingle's bandage. He explored his head gingerly, and Dingle called him a confounded idiot, and cleaned it up and then pronounced Punch's head to be a grade A 1 turnip made of solid Chobham Armour.

'And if I find that Argie who hit me I'll give him a head butt that'll knock his nose through his backside.'

'Sooner him than me.'

The change of plan meant they had to hole up during the day and wait for nightfall before contacting Ickey's patrol. They chose a place where they could go invisible and also keep an eye on the camp. Punch was, as he said himself, highly miffed at missing the ship. The thing was bringing in ammo and grub and reinforcements, and the fact that she was sailing in the Total Exclusion Zone didn't seem to have bothered the Argies.

'They'll use small craft to ferry the stuff across the Sound. Boats they've pinched off the locals as well, more'n likely. Now if we could stop that traffic ...'

'Give you something to do, Punch,' said Dingle. He did not laugh; but humour lurked in his words, despite the pain they all felt at the loss of the Joker.

Death was a fact they all accepted when they signed up for Strike Force.

A few miles off on the other side of the Argentine camp Paul Frost's patrol lay in their hides, completely invisible, and their thoughts hovered on death, the loss of a comrade, the way in which death chose to strike.

Anyone of them could be next.

These four appeared to be poured from the same mould as the rest of Strike Force, some a little taller, others a little shorter, some fuller of face, some lean and evil-looking, others square-cut and craggy. All were hard, tough and not untouched by loss. Each was an individual in his own right, not just a name and a number and a nickname, not just a blur in the eye, but a fully-rounded personality, friendly or mean, infuriating or easy to get along with. Their bodies might have been trained to become flesh and blood machines, their brains into battle computers; their spirits remained free.

As a result Ickey stared over the Argie camp and knew exactly what his comrades in Punch's patrol were feeling right now.

'We oughta go down and mallet 'em tonight, Ickey,' said Corporal Dan Taylor, known as Bunce. 'Let 'em know what's what.'

'Since we've nothing else to do,' added Lance Corporal Joe Snider, called Sniper. He was toting an SLR instead of his old Lee Enfield; but the telescopic sights still enabled him to split hairs at incredible distances.

Huey, Lance Corporal Ralph Hughes, burbled air through his closed lips, catching up on sack time under his poncho.

'If we do,' said Ickey, 'it'll have to be early. They'll sail that ship tonight. Certain to.'

'Earlier the better.' Bunce wiped an oily rag up and down the barrel of his Armalite. He had the horrors about what would happen if he didn't keep the M16 scrupulously clean, occasioned by what had happened to the poor deluded Yanks in 'Nam who'd believed public relations propaganda about their new weapons.

With the dying of the breeze the day dawned with a little mist, a clear fine day of late autumn, so that observation of the camp and ship proved simple. The

72

Argentines had made some shifts to camouflage the ship, draping nets and canvas to simulate a rocky outcrop. If a British aircraft happened to fly over, and that was not particularly likely at the moment, the chances were the pilot would be deceived by the camouflage.

During the day Bunce worked obsessively on his Armalite, and Huey woke up to take post. He had an Uzi. Paul Frost was not the only one in Strike Force to think twice about the major's dictat on weaponry. Everyone worshipped the major, for he had made SSF into the powerful and elite force it truly was, even if, right now, it was scattered all over the Falklands to hell and high water.

'Let each man choose the weapon best suited to him,' Major Dan Granville had said, and that was that.

All the same, Ickey Frost tended to agree with Captain Tom Burnaby that it would be nice if they all had weapons that could shoot the same ammo. The answer to that was that in a fight each bloke was on his own, and he could carry his own supply of ammo. There was an answer to that, of course ...

Thinking of poor old Jack the Joker Dexter, Ickey Frost put out a hand to touch his own Enfield Individual Weapon. They'd both been convinced by Captain Tom Burnaby's arguments for the new weapon system. Tom had outfitted his own Signals group with the Enfield Weapon System, and some of the other lads in Strike Force had followed suit. After all, the rifle only weighed 3.8 kilos, as against the SLR's weight of 4.3 kilos. Even when you added optical sights and a thirty round magazine, the weight went up to a good bit less than the 5.06 kilos of the SLR. But the weight of the whole caboodle, as Tom was at pains to point out, was not as important as all the other benefits of the Enfield Weapon System.

One of the lads in the group around Tom, Chunky

Tubes, had said: 'It's the same ammo as the Armalite, right? And that just makes little holes in people. It don't stop 'em like the SLR.'

'Wrong, Chunky, and if you've seen a tumble bullet at work you'll know why.' He made a face. 'Nasty, I know, but that result was purely accidental.'

The ammo itself was less than half the weight of the 7.62mm rounds of the bigger rifle, 12 grammes to 25.

'The Individual Weapon is so marvellously manoeuvrable,' said Tom, enthusiastically. 'It's only 785mm long, instead of 1140mm. They're making a few alterations to the production models; but essentially this is the boy the army will be using in the future.'

'Not me,' said Chunky Tubes. 'I nearly took me nose orf!'

Patiently, Burnaby pointed out that with a bullpup design, with the magazine and breech behind the trigger action, ejection was going to be close to the flier's face. The rounds went out squarely instead of at the SLR's more angular ejection. 'You don't think the designers are going to be daft enough to put out a bondouk that ejects the spent cases up your nostrils, do you? Come on, Chunky!'

'We-ell – it'll take getting used to.'

'No left-handed bloke can shoot it, that's for sure,' was a comment pointed out with some fervour.

'I'll keep me old Lee Enfield,' Sniper said, and went off to find the equivalent of the NAAFI.

Ickey and the Joker had stayed to listen to Burnaby.

It all boiled down to the British Army finally being equipped with an automatic instead of single shot rifle that met with the authorities' approval. The rifle was of British design, originating with the bullpup put which was developed just after the war and which had not been taken up. Instead everyone had gone for the Belgian FN.

As Burnaby said, 'She *looks* such a beautiful job!'

74

Pugsy, who was Burnaby's Signals sergeant, said, 'You've sold me, Tom.' He laughed. 'And I can tell Sasha all about it with absolute security.'

Sasha was Pugsy's dog, whom he worshipped and whom he talked about incessantly. Ickey could remember Pugsy standing there with Tom Burnaby, holding the new rifle, and talking about his dog Sasha.

The light was beginning to go over the firing range and the shadows lengthened. A little breeze began to drift in with a chill. Burnaby finished up by saying that the new Individual Weapon – the IW – was known as XL70E3. They'd made the magazine compatible with the M16A1. The production model's forestock, beside coming in a fancy khaki colour instead of black, had a horizontal grip-ridge instead of vertical grooves. The butt itself was a trifle more chunky, and the machine gun version, the Light Support Weapon, XL73E2, had a twin-wire shoulder extension, plus a rear pistol grip, a bipod and a longer barrel. 'So,' said Burnaby, 'you know my views.'

Then Guy called out to Noggy to get a wiggle on, Smyjo wanted to know where his cane was, the Whizz Kid went past draped in his infernal devices, Q became inquisitive about ammunition expenditures, the day was dying, and they all felt the time had come to leave the firing range and head for home. Ickey and the Joker told Burnaby they'd put in for the IW. All that seemed one hell of a long time ago now to Ickey Frost, one hell of a long time ... Yet it wasn't really. The Falklands nonsense had blown up like a typhoon, and it had been all systems go to get down south.

Well, now, here he was and on recce patrol, and Jack the Joker Dexter had bought it. Bunce, who was on watch, called in a voice that just carried far enough, 'Ickey. Look.'

At that selfsame instant, SS, who was also on watch,

called, 'Punch. Look.'

Punch, like Ickey, rolled to the obbo point and looked down. 'That's it! We're going in – *now!*'

Chapter Nine

The real, as distinct from the pictured thing or event is so different as to be devastating.

You can see a TV picture or film of a motorway at night with the streams of lights, the gold-flinging reflections, the ruby eyes all pouring along like blood corpuscles. You can see a beautiful postcard of Beachy Head.

But – you stand on the island in the centre of a motorway. You stand on Beachy Head. Brother! The real is so shatteringly *more* of everything that there is no contest.

Jack the Joker Dexter knew all about *that*.

After that first angry blow, Captain Hector Caldeiro stepped back. Dexter recovered his balance, his face feeling as though Punch had slid a friendly one to his cheek past his guard. He sat on the bed, feet on the floor, and he lifted his head to look at the intelligence officer. This was going to get nasty.

This was going to be for real.

He'd gabbled away for a considerable time to the plump captain, acting the dazed survivor. One precept of resistance training was to say nothing, to remain stumm. If you said anything, even false information, they had an opening and, like a crowbar into an oyster, they'd go whump and you'd crack wide open.

Make up your mind to it, trap shut, take it, and hang on. That was the drill.

Caldeiro put a finger to his thick moustache in a gesture startlingly reminiscent of Smyjo's favourite mannerism.

'It is useless to resist, Englishman. I have been following your exploits with some interest.'

Stumm.

'You escaped from the cave rather splendidly.'

Stumm.

'You did, however, murder some of our soldiers.'

Stumm and double stumm.

An absurd thought occurred to Dexter: he ought to be thinking of *schtumm* instead of stumm.

If this Argie bastard had seen enough films, he ought to get around to saying: 'Ve haf vays of makink you talk.' He bloody-well did have, of course. Dexter was not naive enough to suppose otherwise. He just had to hold on long enough for Punch and Ickey and the patrols to get clear.

Suppose he said he was SBS and the canoe had overturned and his oppo had been drowned and he'd just swum ashore? No. Stumm. That was the answer, at least for the moment. Dexter had his own ideas about when to start lying.

Caldeiro hit him again. This time the blow contained more force. Dexter let himself fall back across the piled sacks. Good old Punch would have let go with a sly one, that time. He hooked the back of his knees on the bed edge and pulled himself up on the sacks. He looked at Caldeiro again. There was great meaning in that stare.

'We know you landed by helicopter. You are foolish to remain silent, Englishman. It is necessary to know how many of you there may be and where you are.'

Stumm.

Dexter figured the plump captain for a chap who was not particularly fit, in command of a bunch of miserable and unwilling conscripts, and therefore probably not able to put up much of a fight. Mind you, the Argies, conscripts or no conscripts, were quick enough to cheer their heads off when their government, whom most of them hated, used armed force to steal the Falkland Islands. When the British took the islands they were repossessing their own property.

This Hector, now, was an entirely different proposition.

Still, he might be more used to breaking prisoners' fingers or bashing them in the kidneys, or doing whatever disgusting tricks he got up to in Argentina's prisons, than fighting someone face to face ...

Under that swathingly thick anorak he'd have a dinky little pistol. Have to think of that, then.

'Speak up, Englishman. My patience is wearing thin.'

Stumm.

Of course, he was speaking in a foreign language, no doubt fed at least partially by films, and so that must account for his mannered delivery.

'How many of you are there on West Falkland?'

Stumm.

Anyway, how the hell could he know the answer to that? The place could be swarming with Special Forces for all Dexter knew.

There had to be a couple of guards standing outside the door. At least two. Possibly more. Any shout and they'd rush in. They'd shoot quickly enough, Dexter didn't doubt it. The buzz was that the Buzo Tactico, the Argie's Special Forces outfit, had simply charged into the Moody Brook barracks at Stanley where they expected to find the small Royal Marine detachment. They'd just busted the doors open, bunged in grenades and then tommy-gunned with wild abandon. No parley, no opening, nothing. Just that maniac rush with grenades and SMGs.

The Jollies weren't there, praise be ...

'You will have to speak eventually, Englishman. There is hope for you.'

Now why doesn't the stupid bugger threaten me with his revolver? fretted Dexter. The quicker he takes that out the quicker we can get this over with!

All the same, it was still ... Stumm.

The plump captain, called, Dexter had picked up, Captain Oliva by Caldeiro, licked his lips, gave a furtive sideways glance at the intelligence officer and shifted on his feet so as to draw attention to what he had to say.

'Englishman, please. Tell the captain. It will be – ah – not pleasant for you if you do not.'

Stumm.

'I do not, Captain Oliva,' rasped Caldeiro in English, "need your assistance.'

It was very clearly Captain Oliva's turn to remain stumm. His face revealed his own feeling of impotence in the presence of this formidable member of the intelligence community. Maybe the days of the Disappeared Ones were only supposed to be over. Oliva clearly felt that he might be due to join them in their mysterious limbo.

Surprising himself, Dexter inwardly promised to go easy on the plump Oliva.

Caldeiro took a short turn up and down the untidy hut. He halted and snapped his boots together before Dexter. As a performance in the past it had no doubt cowed many a poor, damned, quaking innocent.

'We have had reports that your Special Forces have landed all over the islands, beginning on the first of May. I do not intend them to do any mischief here.'

Dexter drew a breath. He was fed up with this. He made up his mind.

'There's nothing I can tell you, even if you offered to shoot me here and now.'

Caldeiro's handsome face broke into a most charming

smile. He changed on the instant. His moods were volatile, one minute up and beaming, the next a power-hungry torturer. That seemed the verdict to Dexter.

'Splendid! So you *can* tell me, after all. Oh, and believe me, Englishman, I shall not hesitate to shoot you. Personally.'

Dexter used a most insulting expression.

Instantly, Caldeiro's whole demeanour changed again. The smile vanished. He looked savage and a flush stained up along his cheeks. He zipped open the anorak all the way and put his right hand inside. Dexter sat relaxed, waiting.

''I shall show you whether I mean what I say!'

Caldeiro ripped out his handgun and pointed it directly between Dexter's eyes.

The melodrama of the situation had no power to move the Joker; it was more like a tuppeny farce as far as he was concerned. He concentrated on the gun, on the Argie's fist, on the distances, the timing …

The auto was a Browning 9mm and Dexter felt a stab of disappointment. He'd have thought this tough security bastard would at least have equipped himself with a fancy gun, like a Walther PPK or its ilk. As it was, here was an automatic like a Browning Hi-Power, just like the automatics used by NATO. Shame, that …

Dexter flinched just as though he'd been shocked out of his skin and flashed up his hand. His fingers abruptly raked forward. The auto's muzzle was only six inches in front of his eyes. His hand smeared down the side of the gun, pushing the safety from off to on.

Caldeiro pulled the trigger all right.

The safety stopped the gun firing.

Then Dexter hit the intelligence captain. He hit him in the gut and on the bridge of the nose as he fell down. In the next moment the auto was in Dexter's fist and aimed at Captain Oliva.

Ostentatiously he hauled the safety off and said: 'One sound, Captain, and your brains splash.'

Oliva swallowed bile.

'No. No – do not shoot me, please –'

'Shut up, then.'

Dexter was shaking. The trembles ran all up his arms and legs, and swivelled his abdomen up and down like that Type 21 Frigate had done on the way south. By the good Lord! That had been a gamble, a foolish, reckless gamble. But it was one he'd seen and taken. Now it was all over. He just had to get himself under control again. God knew what old Punch would say when he told him – if he told him ...

Now he had the gun in his fist and could look at it from the side he saw that it wasn't quite like a Browning as issued to NATO, the British version of which was styled the 9mm Browning self-loading pistol No 2 Mk 1. He knew he was thinking these irrelevant thoughts so as not to dwell on what he'd just done. He had to concentrate on what he intended to do next.

Well, that was damned-well obvious enough ...

'Turn around, Captain.'

Oliva did so and Dexter struck him a shrewd and not unkindly blow alongside the ear.

With much greater appetite, he bent and let Caldeiro have one, in the same place behind the ear, just to keep him slumbering. He put the auto on the sacks and hefted the intelligence officer up. The anorak, already unzipped, came off easily enough, and he ripped open the fellow's blue blazer and put that on first. It fitted quite well. The anorak waited until he had those splendid boots of Caldeiro's off and on his own feet, the socks in particular feeling like a million dollars.

He zipped the anorak up, leaving the hood down. He did not intend to try to talk his way past the sentries at the door. That was probably a task beyond his competence, out of spy romances and stuff like that. He looked meanly at the back of the hut.

A few bangs and crashes, and then a couple of life-like yells of pain would work wonders in the belief department outside.

He gave the wooden wall a thumping great kick where it looked most rotten and fragile, and then he let out a hell of a shriek. He added words after a bit.

'No, no! Stop, stop!'

The wood splintered away. A dim and uncanny daylight filtered in, so he was probably on the shadowed south side of the hut. All the better. The boots fitted well enough, so that was all right. He'd have to leave Oliva's shoe emporium, after all, for these boots were far more sumptuous. He put his head through the hole and squinted around.

All he could see was another hut about ten feet or so off ahead, and the same familiar and already dreadfully dull Falklands scenery to right and left. Well, he was not a political person, having to spend too much time getting on in the army, so he didn't give a damn if he went right or left.

He pulled his head in again, half-turned, let rip a most fiendish scream.

'All right, all right! I'll talk! I'll tell you!'

With that he hopped out through the hole in the wall and belted left handed to the corner of the hut, where he halted and cast a careful look around. That way lay open ground. Dexter paused for a moment before haring back to the right-hand corner. Here the view was more or less the same. Hobson's Choice, then ...

Rather than run back he started off, making for the first scraggy clump of vegetation alongside the granite outcrop some fifty yards off. He walked along erect, not running, acting as though he was an Argie officer out for a prowl around. His back crawled as though spiders were climbing from rump to nape.

The hood was pulled up, so he looked like any other anoraked figure wandering about the Argie camp. At this distance his trousers would look normal to anyone on sentry go. The soldiers of the world's armies tended to look increasingly like each other these days, with obvious exceptions. He carried on walking like Felix, keeping the pace down until he reached the vegetation where he halted and half-turned for a look back.

He could see no one.

If anyone was watching him they might well imagine he was out to relieve himself, although he had no idea of the camp's sanitary arrangements. He dropped into the cover of the vegetation and hugged the ground.

No great hullabaloo started up.

A couple of hundred yards further on, more cover, or what the Falklands considered cover, tempted him. He had to get up, walk nonchalantly across the open ground towards the outcrop, and keep the screaming desire to run like hell well and truly locked away. He felt a trifle warm by the time he flopped into the second group of rocks and looked back.

If he could just contrive to work his way into the little crest line ahead he'd have every chance of getting clear away. Commonsense told him that an Argie seeing him making for the rocks over there would think twice before accepting that he was another Argie. It would depend on who spotted him. A low grade conscript might not even bother his head over the problem, being far more concerned with his next meal and fag. A snappy little NCO might start to bellow and froth at the mouth, imagining perhaps he had a desertion to contend with.

Dexter was not dubbed the Joker for nothing.

He began to swing his arms about. He rotated them forward together and then backwards together, then forward and backwards like windmills' sails. After a bit he started to jog up and down, performing quick little spurts of running, even having the cheek to do a standing sprint, staying on the spot and belting his feet up and down. Through all this pantomime, he moved steadily nearer and nearer the crest line.

He didn't believe in jogging as a way of keeping fit. Blokes tended to fall down with heart-attacks, or it didn't do much for you. Give the exercise the big band sound, go for broke, bash it as hard as you could. Then rest up. If you didn't kill yourself you'd soon notice the difference. Some of the lads disagreed with him on this; right now he didn't give a damn what system the Argies favoured. He had to fool them. He had to keep his cool, put on this act, reach the rocks, and then let all the shakes he was keeping in with such discipline do what they would for a bit.

After that – run like hell.

Carrying on with his pantomime, Dexter moved purposefully towards the cover. Strange how all the training which he had undergone, which he had endured, tended to collide like skyrockets in his head. His own willpower was materially reinforced by training and experience. They said that a battalion's morale sank to zero when they were notified they were on posting to Northern Ireland. One could well understand the reason, having to wander along on patrol and be shot at without shooting back properly. The damned nuisance here was that whilst he could shoot back with everything he had and with every intention of claiming hits, he had only an auto pistol and he had to act as though he was an Argie.

Damned odd ...

Training, willpower, morale ... Dexter did his little sprints and his arm exercises and moved closer to the crest. He knew very well he could not carry on much longer.

Someone, a bossy NCO probably, would bellow out

for him to come back. Or they'd enter the hut and find the two sleeping beauties. Or one of them might wake up; he had not hit Oliva with half the force he'd used on Caldeiro.

When the first shouts lifted and the whistles blew the effect was one of total relief.

He just put his head down and ran for the rocks. He did not run blindly in that desperate dash.

The first bullets began to crack and snap about his flying figure.

Chapter Ten

The Joker's trick had brought him close up to the sloping ground leading up to the crest. A bullet flicked the sleeve of his anorak. He jinked that way automatically. His brain was not functioning on standard time; it was off on its own, disconnected from his control, running his body and ordering events. Time to go to ground.

He hit the deck and a spray of bullets clattered into the rocks past him. A moment later and the machine gun would have chopped him in half.

He swivelled himself around and glared back.

He took out his pistol.

Right, then. If this was it, this was it ...

Men were running out from the huts and tents, waving their arms. They carried weapons. Most of them appeared to be kitted out, although some did not wear helmets and others no equipment. They ran on towards his hiding place.

He lined up the auto. Thirteen shots, and then – blooey!

He could always surrender again.

There again, Captain Hector Caldeiro, fingering the lump on the back of his head, no doubt also annoyed by the loss of his club blazer, would stalk up, swishing his swagger stick. No. No, Dexter didn't fancy that.

The Argies were yelling as they ran on. Well, that might keep up their morale –

A rattle of gunfire broke out just off to his right and

some of the leading Argies fell.

Instantly, Dexter's whole future changed.

Good old Punch! Good old SS and Dingle!

The machine gun opened up again and bullets kicked into the ground a few metres off. That was an Argentine-built 7.62mm FN MAG, and not at all pleasant. He began to wriggle backwards, keeping low.

A 66mm rocket from a LAWs erupted against the side of a hut. The hut began to burn instantly.

The machine gun stopped firing.

One of the lads had spotted the machine gun, then, and put a LAWs into it. Splendid stuff! And, in addition, nasty and dangerous and highly lethal.

He just wanted to get out of here.

A straggly clump of orange-brown vegetation afforded a breathing space, and he halted and looked back.

The Argentine soldiers, on coming under attack, had very sensibly stopped running forward. Some of them dropped flat. Others ran away. Some appeared dazed.

A man waving his arms, gesticulating, was clearly an officer attempting to drive them on.

A spatter of rifle shots from the rocks to his right was followed by the collapse of the Argie officer. He just dropped his pistol and fell down.

Dexter found himself hoping that wasn't Captain Oliva.

At that the rest of the Argie soldiers decided that discretion ruled, and started back for their camp. Only a few shots followed them, more to keep the wind up their tails than from any more hostile intent.

Dexter stood up and started off towards his comrades at a brisk trot.

The first thing Punch said was: 'Glad you've decided to rejoin, Joker. Now you can carry your own bleeding kit.'

'What there is of it,' amplified SS, 'the rest's back there.'

'Oh,' said Dingle, 'we can pick that up later.'

'Nice line of outfitters they've got down there,' said Punch. He stared at Dexter's boots. 'Nice boots.'

'You keep your thieving eyes off these boots – not that they'd fit your great plates of meat.'

'What happened to your face?'

'Argie wanted some punch-bag practice.'

'Like that, was it?'

'Yeh. Where's Ickey?'

'About to blow a hole in their damned ship, I hope and trust.'

Punch, then, Dexter noticed, was still talking. Only then did the big CSM mention anything about the situation at hand.

'Hey, Joker! Can you hack it?'

'Wanta punch on the nose, Punch?'

'Right. Let's go give Ickey a hand.'

The terrain over which he now marched, the rocks, the vegetation, the very dank wet taste of the air, the smell of the sea – all these sensory impressions came to Dexter with a new and wonderfully refreshing reassurance. He was back among his comrades. He was no longer in mortal danger of his life. He could look forward to a brew up and a bite to eat.

Of course he was hungry; he'd just had to shove that away somewhere where it didn't bother him.

As for being tired; he'd had a good rest after he'd staggered out of the sea. And tiredness was, until you reached virtually the end of your tether, a state of mind.

Punch said: 'We saw your antics, Joker. Clever.'

'Muscular contractions.'

There was no doubt that the big fellow knew what Dexter was talking about. He could understand. The feeling that at any moment a bullet could whistle in and shatter your spine, blow your head off, could maim you for life if it didn't kill you, was one to conjure with. Oh, yes, Punch Fuller knew all about that.

What, wondered Dexter, would Punch make of his antics in the kelper's hut when that bastard Caldeiro had held a gun at his head?

There had been absolutely no use in trying for the forearm deflection to push the gun aside. Caldeiro would have been ready for that one, and would either have drawn back or shot. As it was, Dexter's hand had whipped up high, as though in prayer – that was probably what Caldeiro had thought at the time.

He'd enjoy that. He'd freak out on a victim praying for help. Dexter's hand, above the automatic, had given Caldeiro no cause for alarm until the moment the harsh fingers swept in and switched the safety to off.

Dexter felt the warmth of the moment, the feelings in him, his driving obsession to get the cat and mouse game over with. That moment would stay with him for a long long time – until he died.

Of course, Hector Caldeiro and torturers like him weren't worth a mouseturd each. Any thoughts of revenge were childish nonsense. He supposed that there must be a lot of other men in Argentina called Hector Caldeiro who were good, honest, upright citizens, decent sorts of fellows, whose misfortune was to have a blight like his inquisitor bearing their name.

Punch carried out a beautiful tactical advance over that section of the terrain. It was daylight, and the sun shone with a brightness no one could have expected so far south at this time of the year. Punch led them from cover to cover. They were out of sight of the camp here, but there was no telling when an Argie patrol might suddenly pop over a crest line. Dexter wished he could make up his mind if the Argies would chase after them or not. If it was left up to Oliva, assuming he hadn't been shot, there probably would be no pursuit, or no hard-pressed chase.

Hector Caldeiro would pursue venomously.

If Punch's scheme worked then turdhead Caldeiro would go after them in the wrong direction. They circled the camp and came around again to the sea, where SS crawled forward to take a dekko. His left hand abaft the seat of his trousers lifted and the finger crooked. Punch grunted and the three inched up alongside SS.

Ickey showed himself for a flashing instant of movement between rocks and then vanished.

'Naughty, naughty,' said Punch.

Dexter looked more closely.

'Nope, Punch. Only way he could get there and there aren't any Argies in his line of sight.'

'Yeh.'

The sea looked unappetising, although it was blue enough, with sparkles and ripples glinting. Dexter could still feel those clamping constrictions of cold upon his body. His whole attitude to swimming could become psychologically blighted if he didn't watch it. Thinking these inane thoughts provided an escape valve for his feelings.

Punch flipped out his Scimitar and called, 'Ickey? Punch.'

'Yeah, this is Ickey,' came the reply. 'How's the Joker?'

'Fine.'

'The ship's still here, hidden. I'm moving into range now.'

Further along the beach around the cove bend, the humped and twisted, grained-white and black-shadowed pile of canvas covering the ship was just about within rocket range. There was no sign of movement there. No doubt everyone had gone running back up to the camp to find out what all the excitement was about. Then they'd be organized into search parties to chase the Special Forces Brits.

'Yeh,' said Punch. 'Can see. We'll cover you coming

out.'

'Check.'

Punch stowed away the Scimitar.

The 66mm rocket projectile from the LAWs should punch through the plating of the ship without any trouble. She was not an armoured warship, after all — and were there any armoured warships left in the world? Well, yes; but they were in mothballs. Dexter didn't doubt that his own attempt had been worthwhile. This way of going about the task was undeniably more hazardous.

They watched as Ickey's patrol closed, and they rarely spotted the camouflaged forms. At last Ickey came on the air and said, 'It's go.' He went off and the next instant a smashing concussion from the side of the ship indicated the dance had commenced.

Ickey Frost's patrol did not have to face the icy horror of the water; they did have to hightail it back to safety before they had their heads blown off.

They let the ship have three more LAWs and then started back. Carefully watching the approach from the camp, Dexter saw no movement there. Punch, too, spotted the obvious. He ripped the little wireless set out.

'Ickey! There's no one. Run for it!'

Soon four lithe figures were breaking cover below and running hard up from the beach.

They'd just about reached the clumps of vegetation where Punch's patrol lurked when a figure appeared hanging over the rail of the ship's side. Canvas drooping down over the deck had no doubt prevented him from getting there sooner. He could be the captain, he could be the cabin boy left on watch. Strike Force didn't know.

SS lined up his rifle and let one go.

The figure by the rail slumped.

'Those bangs'll bring 'em in any second.' Punch stood up. 'Come on you lot! Let's leg it!'

Running and leaping over the ground, avoiding rocks, haring for it, eight figures legged it away.

Breath harsh in the throat, feet thumping, head down yet eyeballs scouring the way ahead, arms holding in yet balancing each lunging stride, the eight men of Stike Force fled.

Their line of retreat had to pass by way of their cached kit; this was achieved without incident, for no Argies had stumbled across the hidden rucksacks. The jaguar packs went on their backs, the valises were snatched up, Dingle hoisted the big wireless set and they were ready. This time they'd go into cover far more cautiously.

Ickey's gear, cached separately, was also picked up without incident.

The distant droning, as of a fly against a window pane, told them they'd only barely made it.

'I,' said Punch with some acerbity, 'could do with a Blowpipe right now.'

'Yeah,' said Ickey. 'And you can carry it.'

They had no flak equipment with them. Against aircraft, they could only shoot their small arms and hope. Normally they'd got to ground, hide, and hope the buggers wouldn't see them and just fly away.

They selected a good spot where a gulley enabled them to spread their ponchos and so construct quite a capacious hide beneath. Dexter badly wanted a brew up; that would have to wait. They positioned the big wireless sets away from each other. One potential hit wasn't going to knock out all their communications gear ...

Dexter applied an eyeball to a gap and surveyed the sky. The droning sound swelled.

'Bleeding Pucara, I bet,' said SS.

'Likely,' agreed Bunce.

'Two of 'em,' suggested Sniper.

'Half a dollar on it?'

'Make it a bar,' said Huey. 'I feel lucky.'

Dingle said: 'You're on.'

'Make it two,' said Bunce. 'We'll take your lolly any time.'

Ickey Frost's contribution was to say: 'I'm not taking any bets on how long that freighter took to sink.'

'Sitting on the bottom, I bet,' said Huey. 'Wanta take a fiver on it? Check when we get back?'

The others ignored this. Dexter's viewpoint, restricted as of necessity by the angle of the boulders, showed blue sky with those Falkland-style puffs of cloud. The planes appeared overhead, whistled past and were gone.

'Well?' demanded Bunce.

Dexter let them hear a nasty little snigger, which he could put on for effect to perfection.

'You lose.'

'Then we win,' said SS.

'Nope.'

'Huh?'

'Three.'

'Why,' broke out SS in a most menacing fashion, 'the thieving, conniving bastards!'

'Yeah — and two's nearer three than one,' said Sniper. 'So we win, anyways.'

'Nah —'

'We'll settle this later, and I really feel sorry for you lot!'

So, in a happily combative frame of mind, the two patrols settled down.

There would be no more daylight movement for them now the Argies had brought up such formidable aerial reinforcement. In the ordinary course of this little exercise, Dexter wouldn't believe the Argies could spare three aircraft to search for the Brits. That must be quite a proportion of their total aerial strength here in West Falkland. There were other parties of British Special Forces ashore, scouting, carrying out recces, doing the odd

94

nasty malletting every now and again. To whistle up three Pucaras like that told Dexter one very important fact – a fact he already suspected.

Captain Hector Caldeiro, intelligence officer, was a very influential person indeed.

'They ought to be back in a coupla hours,' said Punch. 'After they've been briefed.'

'Reckon more like three,' said Bunce. 'They can't be all that smart, can they? I mean, Pucaras, and over here on West Falkland.'

'Don't –' began Dexter.

SS cut in fiercely, smarting under the last fiasco of the betting fraternity.

'We'll say two or under, Bunce. You say three. How about a fiver on that?'

'Done.'

'It's in the bag.'

Dingle said: 'I'm in for half, SS.'

So, happily wrangling about the prospective time before their enemies would fly out to search for them to kill them, the two patrols of Strike Force settled back once more.

Some of the lads would bet on the direst outcomes. Like the time Roger Rawson had been in schtuck with that foreign bird, the lads had bet vastly and with great gusto on the outcome. Poor old Romeo had handled himself well, though, give him credit for that. Roger Rawson, initials RR, had been dubbed Romeo Romeo for the international call and, also, because he had black crinkly hair, a winning smile with two real unashamed dimples, and fancied himself a ladies' man.

Then they'd bet on how many bones Sapper Jones had busted when his chute failed to open properly.

Pugsy had guessed it to within one bone short and he'd gone around to the hospital to plead with Sapper just to let him bust a little finger bone – not much – so's he could scoop the pool. Sapper had managed to indicate that Pugsy could hightail it out of the dock. Still, it was a thought, and the lads gave Pugsy credit for initiative.

Dingle called up HQ to report.

Punch said: 'Tell Shrimp to gee up whoever's taking us out.'

After a lengthy conversation, Dingle sat back.

'Shrimp says they're so short on choppers it isn't true. If we can join up with Rommel's patrol they'll try to get us off as a single chunk.'

Punch looked disgusted.

'We'll have to cut inland to get across to Rommel. No way of going around the coast line.'

'That's the idea.'

'Better than sitting here,' contributed Ickey.

'Yeh,' said Dexter.

Rommel was the only obvious name for Derek Anthony Kershaw, particularly as he had joined Strike Force from a tank regiment, and he'd muttered dark thoughts about swiping a Scorpion or a Scimitar from the Blues and Royals.

'Might come in handy,' he'd said.

No one poo-poohed the idea.

Now Punch and Ickey's patrols had to hack it inland, curving around the coast where the Argies would be out looking for them after their reconnaissance of those areas, and join up with Rommel. After that, they might stand a chance of being lifted off.

As Dexter said, voicing all their thoughts, 'What'll happen when we get there is that they'll ask us to swim out.'

'Didn't bring me water wings,' said Huey.

'One thing,' said Punch in his new expansive way of talking. 'The old Joker's had a little practice swim already.'

'They can send *Invincible* for me,' said Dexter. 'Or I ain't going!'

Chapter Eleven

When Punch and Dexter went around to Day's Fish Parlour on the evening of the day following the funeral, they found the shop busy, and Sam and his parents fully occupied.

The smell of fish, which usually upset Dexter, was not anywhere near as bad when it was fish and chips, and the spicy scents of vinegar ameliorated much of what would otherwise have been unpleasant.

'You can't get the old rock salmon like you us'da,' complained Punch. 'Or a really decent piece of cod.'

For Punch, that was a speech.

'Here's a nice piece,' said Mrs Day, expertly sliding the fish out and onto the greaseproof paper. It did look good, Punch agreed. Chips followed in their own paper bag. 'One thing,' went on Mrs Day. 'Chips are no good if you wrap 'em up and keep them too long. Eat them now, that's best.'

Dexter cleared his throat, knowing he was going to utter what amounted to blasphemy.

'I'd like a beef and onion pie, please, Mrs Day.'

'Very well, dear.'

They were not far enough North to be in the area of mushy peas. They took their purchases and looked around. Sam studiously ignored them. Harriet was nowhere to be seen.'

'Ah – Harriet in?' said Dexter.

'No. She's still upset, poor thing. Well – aren't we all –'

Dexter waited.

After a bit, Mrs Day said: 'Harriet's gone round to see her friend Mildred. Nice girl.'

They secured the address, thanked Mrs Day, and went out eating their fish and chips and pie and chips from the paper. The food was good, no doubt about that. Trade was brisk. The shop must take a tidy sum each evening.

'That's gotta be the answer, Punch,' said Dexter, swallowing down the last of the beef and onion pie. He had a few chips left, and he jealousy guarded them from Punch, who'd reach over and help himself if an opening was made available.

'Yeh.'

'If Harriet is too frightened to talk –'

'She will be.'

'So we have to try to persuade her. It won't be easy.'

'Nope.'

Mildred's house was just another small terraced building in a row, with a miniscule front garden and, at the back, a patch where her father attempted to grow beans and onions, with a few tomatoes under glass. The house was freshly painted. The evening smells were pleasant, and lights were coming on in windows along the street.

Mildred herself opened the door and immediately looked alarmed. She flinched back and tried to slam the door shut.

Dexter said: 'Mildred? We're friends of Ernie's. We'd like to see Harriet –'

'Clear off! You rotten – clear off or I'll call the cops!'

Harriet's voice floated from the passage.

'Mildred! Please –'

Dexter called: 'It's us, Harriet, Mr Fuller and Mr Dexter. We want to talk to you.'

When Harriet had assured her friend that these two hulking great brutes were friends of Ernie's, the situation eased. Mildred was a well-built girl, busty, with excellent teeth that in ordinary circumstances would have been revealed a lot when she smiled. Now her eyes were red and her face lumpy from crying. She wore a neat blue and white dress, and shoes whose heels were just the right height. Dexter thought he read the situation, and chanced his arm.

'We were good mates with Ernie, Mildred. We don't like what happened. If you liked him ...'

She put a lace handkerchief to her mouth. After a bit, she managed in a choked voice to say: 'Yes. I liked Ernie.'

Harriet, pale and apprehensive, closed the door, ushering Punch and Dexter into the front parlour. Mildred was clearly close to tears once more. Her parents were out, and Harriet had come around; but no one could tell who was giving comfort to whom. It was reciprocal, that was for sure.

Harriet confirmed Dexter's thoughts by saying, 'It's no real secret, Mr Dexter. Mildred and Ernie were walking out. What do you want to ask me?'

'First thing, Harriet, we don't want to upset you —'

'Upset me!'

'Yes, I know. But —'

'Does Sam know you're here?'

'I don't think so. Your mother told us, and Sam was busy. Nice little trade at your dad's shop.'

'Yes!' she flared, and the bitterness was patent. 'Nice little business. And they wanted their share —'

'Ah!' said Punch, and relapsed into silence.

Harriet's eyes widened.

Dexter said: 'So it was the protection racket. Now, Harriet, if Ernie wouldn't play along, and it wasn't an accident, then ... Well, you tell us who, and —'

'And you'll end up with your face in the fryer!'

Dexter had to be patient.

'Sam is frightened, well, that's fair enough. He has to live here. And it's clear how far they'll go. I suppose Ernie found out and told them to clear off.'

'Yes.' Harriet slumped into the armchair. She was shaking. Her face drained of blood. Dexter felt such a flood of sympathy for her, such a flood of savage anger for the bastards who'd done this to the Day family, that he had to take a conscious grip on himself.

'You might as well tell us, Harriet.'

Mildred cut in to say: 'You in the army, too?'

'Yeh.'

'I was so proud of Ernie when he came home to show us his wings and his red beret. You ...?'

'Yeh.'

'They started at fifty a week, and then it went up to seventy-five.' Harriet sat erect. Mildred perched on the arm of the chair and the two girls gripped each other's hands. Dexter just concentrated on what Harriet was saying.

'Seventy-five.'

'Yes. They'll put it up to a hundred soon.'

Supposing, Dexter reasoned, a bloke could earn seven or eight thousand a year to keep his family, after his expenses but before tax. The demands on him would be an enormous strain. He could pay, but there'd be only just enough to live on left. These bastards knew how to cut the cloth.

'All right. Now tell us –'

'I don't want you to be – to be –'

'Just tell us all you know.'

What Harriet had to say made Punch, sitting silently, harbour odd thoughts, concerned with tommy guns rattling and grenades going off, with a few redhot stakes thrown in for good measure. Like Dexter, he realized he

100

had to keep his cool. Harriet had been in the next room when the four men entered the shop. She had seen it all. Sam had protested that fifty to seventy-five was too much. Ernie had started to cut up rough, and they'd tried to manhandle him. That was a mistake where a member of Strike Force was concerned.

'Ernie threw one of them down and stopped the next one. I started to think it was going to be all right. Then ...' She stopped, swallowed, tried to speak, sat miserably silent for a moment. Then she burst out: 'Ernie was trying – and one of them came up behind him and hit him on the head with a stick thing. Ernie fell down. It was awful. After that –'

'All right, Harriet. That's enough.'

No need to guess the hideous scene which followed.

'And Sam saw all this?'

She shook her head.

'No. He ran out.'

'Don't blame him.'

'Except for his brother,' said Punch.

'Yeh. Still, Sam's not built for it.'

'These bastards know that. They were scared of Ernie. So they did for him.'

Punch stood up. He looked immense in that neat front parlour.

'All right, Miss Harriet. Now you forget all about it if you can. The Joker'n me take over now.'

Two long speeches in succession from Punch made Dexter realise how much his comrade had been affected. They received adequate descriptions of the men involved, for Harriet didn't know their names, except that one had been called Eddie by his friends. One of them, she also said, wore two-tone shoes.

'They'll hang out in the pub where Sam was, I expect,' said Dexter. 'But I don't know if we need to go find 'em. Maybe it'd be better to let them come to us.'

'Pick our own terrain,' said Punch.

They said goodnight to the two girls, once again telling them to try to put it all out of their minds, which fatuous piece of advice was recognized as such by all, and went off to the local. On the way Punch stopped at a telephone box.

'Gotta tell Barky.'

'Sure.'

'Well?'

Realizing that the big fellow's speeches had returned to their normal length, Dexter called Barky and outlined the situation.

Lieutenant Miles Barker sighed over the phone.

'I suppose you're going in bald-headed, Joker.'

'Why not? The girl can't give evidence in open court against these bastards. If she does, their friends –'

'Yes. It's a damned ugly business. Wait on it tonight. I think some of the lads might be interested.'

'You'll send three and fourpence before we go to the dance?'

'It seems logical.'

'Yeh. I'll try to chain Punch down.'

'Put him on, Joker.'

Dexter didn't hear what Barky said; what Punch said after a bit was: 'All right, Barky. One day.'

He slammed the phone down. His face could have been used to break a channel through to Graham Land.

Instead of saying: 'It makes sense, Punch,' Dexter had sense enough himself to say nothing.

They were used to violence; but the major frequently drummed into them that violence was messy, often unnecessary, and always ugly. This kind of stupid violence, so different from the ordered yet chaotic madness of a battlefield, upset them in a way which surprised even themselves. They could appreciate many soldiers' viewpoint that you respected your opponent, even when both of you were trying to kill the other. But these vermin, they'd murdered Ernie in a hideous way, they knew they had power; their violence could not be condoned on any scale of respect.

They didn't go to the local, after all, and that night Shrimp rang them at their hotel. He told them that a lot of the lads were off on a scheme – he was not more specific. The Welsh Physical had been followed immediately by a leave rota. Nevertheless a gang of the lads was on the way, driving all night.

'Captain Tom Burnaby can't come.' Here Shrimp's voice dropped into a conspiratorial whisper. 'We hear he's hanging around a stripper – but no one has the true gen.'

'Good luck to him,' said Dexter. 'We'll wait.' He looked at Punch as he said this. Punch put his hands behind his head, stretched out on the bed, and stared angelically at the ceiling.

Now, in very much the same attitude, Punch Fuller stared up at the screening ponchos in their hide on West Falkland, and sorted out the best line of march in his mind. The map was branded on his brain. Like the Joker Dexter, he could sense out a line of march. Trouble here was the soft ground, the openness of it all, prowling Argie aeroplanes and helicopters, and the doubtlessly inevitable deterioration of the weather.

He rolled over, pulled the map around, and stuck his hard forefinger down on their present position. He drew his finger inland, turned through forty-five degrees, carried on another forty-five, and then slashed his finger off the map.

'That's it.'

Dexter agreed with Punch's reading of the situation. Ickey Frost pursed up his lips, nodded, and said nothing. So, that was the way they'd hack it.

SS, on watch at the little gap where they'd not fully

fastened the press studs along the reinforced edges of the ponchos, called: 'Chopper.'

They all heard the *chip-chop-chip* in the next instant. Punch tapped SS on the shoulder, and took his place at the spyhole.

'Looking for us.'

Dexter said: 'What about them pesky Pucaras, then?'

'Could be a different op altogether,' said Ickey.

Bunce left off cleaning his Armalite to say, 'It's under two hours, sure. But you don't count the chopper.'

Quite happy to stir with the big wooden spoon, SS said, 'We said they'd be back looking for us in two hours or less, Bunce. Fair's fair.'

'We said them Pucaras!'

The whirring sound passed overhead, and for that moment at least the men of Strike Force had respect enough to remain silent. The slithering sound of the heli's vanes through the air diminished, faded and died.

'Nah,' said Sniper. 'Me and Huey reckon you'll have to get your Pucaras back to win the bet.'

'That chopper's a no-ball,' pointed out Dingle. 'Alters the odds.'

'Get knotted.'

Punch said, 'Wrap it up.'

'You'd never believe looking at you lot,' said Dexter, 'that it takes six months and eight thousand quid to train a para, and then you're just beginning.'

Bunce held his cleaning rag poised over his M16. What he might have said would never be known, for Ickey just gave him a look.

Seeing Bunce at his obsessive task made Dexter realize how pleased he was that Punch and the lads had hung onto his Individual Weapon. He pulled it across and started to check it out, finding as Tom Burnaby had prophesied, the various sub assemblies swift and neat to strip. The whole thing came to pieces, more or less, and

104

he bent his attention to cleaning and making sure everything was AOK. He and Punch kept the specialist night sights, image intensifiers, thermal imagers, separate and for general work Dexter used the supplied Sight Unit Small Arms Trilux, SUSAT. The SUSAT had a times four magnification and needed no maintenance. On the top of the sight unit an ordinary iron sight was also fitted — just in case.

So the eight men of Strike Force out on this recce patrol spent their time under cover through the day, checking weapons, brewing up and eating as best they could, resting, taking post.

The Pucaras did not fly back and great was the wailing and gnashing of teeth in certain quarters under the ponchos.

The helicopter flew over twice more.

'They smell blood,' said Huey.

'I ain't got none to spare,' Sniper told his oppo. 'You'll have to divvy up.'

In the main, though, there was not a great deal of conversation.

The moment Punch deemed the visibility low enough, he started them out. They had a good long hack on tonight, and they humped their loads and spoke sparingly, and hacked on. True enough, they were much lightened now; grub had been eaten, ammo fired away, the plastic and the LAWs all but expended. Because of that Dexter decided to keep the auto he'd taken from Captain Caldeiro. Its weight was a weight to carry; but he was still much relieved from the enormous weights they'd started with.

He was pleased that they didn't have a machine gun with them. Oh, sure, a machine gun would be valuable if they had a biggish firefight on their hands. Their task as a recce patrol was to avoid getting into a fight. A General Purpose Machine Gun weighed in at 11.77 kilos, around twenty-four pounds, and the jimpy, although popular, was an item to lug around. Ollie Oliver, with Number One Wing, was toting a jimpy around, wherever Number One Wing had got themselves to now.

Burnaby had been pleased to point out that the Enfield System machine gun – the Light Support Weapon – weighed under seven kilos. He'd kitted Spider out with one of those in his Signals Group. Maybe, Dexter figured as he humped along under the stars of the Falklands, maybe he ought to have talked Punch into an LSW. Just maybe.

Many thoughts crowded into his brain, and the rhythm of marching blended easily with them. Sometimes he just blanked out on a hack and didn't come to until they'd reached their destination. This night, though, he turned over pleasant carnal thoughts of Patsy. That night her single-strap evening gown had broken that single strap, and he'd had to slip his knife away very sharpish, very sharpish indeed. At the moment he felt more like recalling Patsy, her squeals and the marvellous way she handled the situation, than what had followed on the revelations.

He was just about ready to follow Patsy up the hotel foyer and into the lift when Punch stopped dead.

Against the sky ahead of them flame licked up, orange and fanlike, and died away, to bloom once again.

Very, very faintly they could hear the little popping sounds.

'That's a fight up there,' said Punch.

'And it'll be Rommel, for sure,' Ickey swore. 'Hell! and we're miles away yet!'

About to suggest they dump all non-essential kit and get across there as fast as they possibly could, Dexter saw the flashes in the sky fade away, heard the tiny crackle of sound die.

'It's one way or the other.' Punch ripped out his

Scimitar. 'Rommel! Come in, Rommel!'

The little radio remained obstinately mute.

Again Punch called.

'Nothing,' he said at last. 'Right. We'll go over there and see the damage. Gawd 'elp the Argies if Rommel and his patrol have bought it!'

Chapter Twelve

Ickey Frost marched into the foyer of the hotel with such a grim and menacing expression that Punch had to say: 'Ease up, Ickey. You'll frighten the poor barmaid's knickers off.'

'Afterwards,' said Ickey.

He was followed by Dingle who, at the mention of barmaids, licked his lips and said, 'They've gotta be open here, right? It's a hotel, ain't it?'

'Pints all round,' said Punch. 'Then fish and chips.'

'Suits me.'

They were all wearing casual civilian clothes, windcheaters in a variety of ultra-modern patterns, jackets, slacks; once they had a pint inside them they relaxed enough to carry out their proper job and melt into the scenery.

'Barky was most emphatic,' Ickey told Dexter and Punch. 'We have to stay inside the law. If –'

'If the law can't help the Days ...' began Dexter, hotly.

'It can if we give it leverage. We have to persuade these turdheads to leave the Days alone. We may have to be rough on 'em ...'

'Too right!'

'– and if we get a reasonable amount of evidence, they could be convicted, and we'd give evidence, and not young Harriet.'

'That seems sound.'

'Y'know what the major says – violence breeds violence. We use kid gloves ...'.

'Oh, come *on*, Ickey!'

'... until we have to mallet 'em.'

'That's more like it,' said Punch.

The shop appeared to be very little different from the previous evening. A small area off to the side of the entrance provided space for four tables, each with four chairs, bright red-and-white checked. The noxious head of VAT reared itself at the counter, and was dissipated if you sat down and ate your fish and chips *in situ*. Punch ordered, and half-turned to Dexter, 'Beef and onion?'

'Yeh.'

The plates provided were of white china, uncracked. The cutlery, of that stainless steel variety given away at petrol pumps, was shining and immaculately clean. Dexter started carving his pie as the others dissected their fish.

No one left any chips within spitting distance of Punch. Even so, he snaffled two from Dingle and popped them into his craggy mouth with the triumphant air of a man making an eagle at the tricky seventeenth.

'You,' Dingle told Punch morosely, 'have got hollower legs than Trampas.'

They'd left their visit late enough so that they could reasonably still be finishing their meal at closing time. Sam kept on shooting uneasy glances in their direction; but they were quiet, behaving themselves, and not even drinking. If Harriet's information was accurate, then just after Sam turned the OPEN/CLOSED sign over on the glass door the expected company would arrive.

Half past ten came and went and Sam did not flip the sign.

'Come on, Sam. Close up.'

'Just waiting for you to leave –'

'Close up!'

Sam burst out, eyes liquid, face red, scared right down to his underpants and rightfully so. 'What can you *do*? They'll get me – they've promised! Just go away ...'

Dingle stood up, walked to the door and flipped the sign. Mr and Mrs Day retired reluctantly. There was a great deal of Ernie's get up and go in the old man; but age and responsibility had worn the older man down. A few words were exchanged, mainly to do with keeping Harriet out of trouble, and then Sam, for whom the men of Strike Force felt profoundly, looked out the window and said, 'Here they come.'

Three of them were the three they'd seen in the pub when Sam had incontinently run off. One was as big as Punch, an ex-pug probably, and more than likely both punch-drunk and a half-wit who bashed people to order.

The middle-sized one with his hideous two-tone shoes and sharp suit looked as though he could be useful; and his swagger was all the more unpleasant.

The smallest of the three seemed to belong to that weasel-ilk who run and fetch and carry and tattle tales, who fawn and flatter. Dangerous, though, and probably with a flick-knife in his jeans.

The fourth – and he might well be Eddie, guessed Dexter – appeared to be the leader from the way the others treated him. His face was broad and florid, well-used, his hair fair and crinkly. His suit was expensive, he wore a great deal of gold in cuff links and chains and wristwatch, and if there was a bulge under his left armpit – well, that had to be filed away under information to be assessed and dealt with.

They didn't waste time.

Eddie, the weasel and the pug lounged a little in the background as two-tone shoes pushed up to the counter and spoke to Sam.

'Hullo, Sam. How y'do doing?'

'Look – Jim – I'm –'

110

'Hand it over, Sam, now. Right away. Savvy?'

They took no notice of the four sitting at the table. They were just men doing a job, minding their own business. No one could take offence at their quiet attitude, the way they didn't smoke in the fish and chip shop, the soft and polite way in which they spoke.

All Sam had to do was open the till and take out seventy-five pounds and hand it over. That was all. He opened the till.

Punch couldn't hold still any more.

He stood up. He walked quietly over to the counter alongside two-tone shoes Jim.

'Having trouble, Sam?'

'No – no trouble –'

If Sam had gone on to plead with Punch to go away, Dexter didn't know what might have occurred. The situation abruptly hung little white-hot spots of fire all over the fish parlour. At once the leader, this flashy Eddie, sized up what was what. Dexter had no real knowledge of gang leaders in the urban situation; but he guessed that a fellow didn't get into the position of capo without having some physical and mental powers. This Eddie would be hot stuff. He would, as the slang had it, have done his Heavy Work to Make His Bones. Probably. The truth was more likely to be that he was a local bad-boy turned hoodlum, able to use force through his friends and associates, and trying to act the big time.

Eddie moved across and said, 'No business of yours, friend. Sam here owes me a loan. Now he repays me That's all.'

'Nope,' said Punch, and for all the world his words ground out like iron ore going through a crusher. 'Nope. There is no debt. Shove off. Leave Sam alone.'

Eddie smiled with that widely-handsome flash of his teeth, that backward cock of the head so the crinkly hair nodded, that charming wrinkling up of the eyes that

111

must have assisted him in conquests and smoothed over innumerable awkward decisions.

'You're out of you depth, friend.'

The true miracle was that Punch still stood there, quivering, it is true, but he remained standing with one hand on the counter – and he did not rip this Eddie's head off and toss it into the fish fryer.

Weasel ran outside.

Two-tone shoes Jim squeaked out: 'This is a set-up! The bastards – you'll get broken legs for this, Sam!'

Eddie's smile remained, wide and fixed. He called out in a penetrating voice: 'Blocker!'

The pug bounced forward, eager, a lop-sided smile giving him the look of a Labrador jumping for a biscuit held in the hand of his master. 'Kin I hit 'im now, Mr Eddie?'

'Back off, friend,' said Eddie. 'Or Blocker will rearrange your features.'

Dingle and Ickey sitting at the table edged forward, legs braced back, ready to take off. It seemed now that a fight would not be avoided. Dexter lined up his target – Eddie the lad himself – and prepared to jump.

Eddie gave an impatient snap of the fingers forward, a contemptuous order to Blocker to go in and bash this stupid obstinate idiot. Blocker surged forward, fists up. He did not have the advantage of being trained up in the unarmed discipline favoured by Strike Force – *keninja* – and therefore it came as a surprise, a catastrophic surprise, to him to find himself flying upside down through the air. He landed on his back with an almighty crash.

As Dexter went over the table headlong for Eddie, Ickey started for two-tone shoes Jim. Dingle yelped out about blighters poaching his territory, and Eddie ripped out a revolver from under that tailored suit and fired a shot that cracked past Punch's ear. Dexter, hurdling the table, saw the gun swivel and he went on low and fast, diving hard.

Dingle's blinding changed to a bull roar.

'Look out! Door! Shotgun!'

Everybody reacted in their own different ways. Dexter, rolling forward to grab Eddie, went on, getting the man's ankles in his fists and yanking savagely. Ickey put a fist into Jim's face and then went on with the blow. Dingle, without cover and isolated, backpedalled fast. Punch picked up Blocker and held him upside down like a shield.

Weasel returned with two more men, each quite openly carrying a sawn-off. No doubt the plastic wrappings had been thrown down just outside the door.

'Stand still,' said Weasel. 'Let Mr Eddie up.'

Dexter's fists had moved from ankles to knees as Eddie, prostrate on the floor, yelled in pain.

Punch yelled, too. He bellowed, 'All out, lads!'

And, with that, he threw Blocker at the two shotgun-men.

There was only one way to go.

One after the other, the four members of Strike Force hurled themselves through the window. Flying glass and splinters of wood spraying, they burst through. They hit the pavement running. Even then, the two gunmen did not shoot Blocker. They lost time avoiding him, and ran for the window. The sawnoffs blasted; but Strike Force was gone.

Chapter Thirteen

If you're too good at life's problems people are just as suspicious of you, although in a slightly different way, as they are if you're no bloody good at all. Major Dan Granville had hand-picked the best for his Special Strike Force; but there are bests and bests in any man's army.

If Rommel had come unstuck up ahead no one was going to blame him, for they all knew how frighteningly easy it was to foul up. All the same, few would be surprised that Rommel was in schtuck.

The flashes of gunfire died and the sounds of a gun battle ceased. The two patrols hacked on. They were determined to find out what had been going on before the sun rose.

Dexter the Joker did not forget he was still wearing Captain Hector Caldeiro's fancy blue blazer.

This recce patrol had not turned out as anyone had expected. It had not all been disaster. They'd put a small freighter on the bottom, and that should help to disrupt supplies for the Argies. They'd recced the beaches assigned to them. They'd reported in to HQ. So far so good.

But he'd like to know what those three Pucaras were up to. There was the injury to Punch's head, which might not have cleared up as beautifully as Punch imagined. And there was the unpalatable fact that Caldeiro was pursuing them with particularly unpleasant designs in that sleekly handsome head of his.

As for Derek Anthony Kershaw, known as Rommel, he'd obviously stirred up another hornet's nest ahead of them. If they weren't light on their feet they could well be caught between two fires.

When Rommel finally came on the air in reply to Punch's call he brushed aside the firefight as a mere inconvenience.

'Ran across a couple of Argies who wouldn't get out of the way, that's all.'

'We're coming in, Rommel. So scrape the eyeballs.'

'Check.'

When one party met up with another party, extra vigilance had to be maintained. Stood to reason, didn't it? And Dexter didn't mind admitting he'd scrape an extra eyeball where Rommel was concerned.

Just how many Argies had got in Rommel's way, then?

Something Rommel hadn't told them, which they found out when the two parties met up, was that two of his patrol had been wounded.

Even with Punch in this loquacious mood he pursed up his lips at the news and refrained from comment. Corporal Dusty Miller had taken one through his left arm, and Acting Corporal Zeb Barnes one through the leg. The wounds in themselves were no more serious than any damned wound; but all kinds of complications might ensue if the lads did not receive early and expert treatment. Funny things happened to arms and legs with bullets through them if the fates did not smile.

The fourth member of Rommel's patrol, Lance Corporal Woody Woods, had come in for more than his share of load carrying as a result of the casualties. He was not overly tall for a craggy member of Strike Force; but he was wide. His shoulders were, as the saying has it, broad enough to carry the burdens imposed on him. He came from Birmingham and his accent, which he tried to alter, delighted his comrades. Dexter, to whom all men of Strike Force were comrades, was glad Woody hadn't copped one.

They now had three of the big Scimitar sets between them. Although dubbed big in comparison to the pocket Scimitars, the long-range sets were still considerably smaller and lighter than the standard issue. They called out HQ and Shrimp told them that transport had finally been arranged.

'Although it'll have to be a double lift. Just aren't enough helis.'

'Wounded and children first,' grunted Punch.

Dexter glanced at his oppo. The big fellow was in good form, then, thanks be; the effects of that bash on the head were presumably fading.

'They're flying in tomorrow night. We've another day stuck here.'

All the men in the hide knew that other men would be sticking their necks out tomorrow night to lift the three patrols of Strike Force off West Falkland. They did not make light of other folks' problems; but Strike Force must come first as far as they were concerned.

By this time in the recce they were raspy of jaw and unwholesome in general appearance. Another day and night to be lived through and then they could look forward to showers and soap and water – hot if the ship's boilers hadn't blown up – and a square meal instead of arctic rations or g-rats.

Dexter found himself wondering how Hector Caldeiro was getting on along the backtrail.

One thing was for sure – he'd travel by chopper. There'd be no yomping for the Argie Intelligence Officer.

One item of information passed on by Shrimp from HQ, regarding the shortage of helicopters, did little to cheer up the men of Strike Force in their damp and boggy hide on West Falkland. Colonel Rygel Cooke, running the Special Evaluation Squadron, had pre-empted the chopper earmarked by HQ. Colonel Rygel Cooke's SES often worked with Colonel Zit Armstrong's SAG – the unit was then referred to as SESAG – and they held their opinion of Major Dan Granville's SSF. They'd done a few ops together and co-operated well; but the spirit of rivalry flared brightly.

Number Four Wing of Strike Force had also been urgently calling for a heli, and they had to be looked after.

As for Number One Wing with the major, Shrimp sounded decidedly odd about them ...

Well, everybody had a job to do, and they were all getting on with it in their various ways. Soon the Falklands would be crawling with British Special Forces. The Argies wouldn't know if they were punched or bored. When the Task Force finally arrived and made up its mind whereabouts it was intending to land, the ground should be nicely softened up. That, at least, was the theory.

Life, at least in Strike Force, it seemed to Punch Fuller, mainly consisted of hiding in wet holes in the ground.

This was absolutely true. The moments of action, when they arrived in splatterings of flame and hideous noise, turned the old insides over a treat and made up for all the wet and boggy holes in the world, let alone in the Falklands.

As for the old Joker, well, Punch considered, he was a mate worth having. He supposed girls had friendships of a similar kind, devoid of all sexual undercurrents. Devoid! The idea of queerly cuddling up to the Joker made Punch feel that the exercise was totally unnecessary. He didn't doubt that most, if not all, blokes had buried homosexual tendencies; but somehow or other a fellow just didn't have the right curves in the right places to turn on Punch Fuller. There were no homosexuals in Strike Force as far as Punch knew, and even if there had been it wouldn't matter outside the blokes concerned, being their business.

Thinking about girls could make a fellow fretful when there weren't any about; but Punch was able to fall into the system practised by many a fighting man sitting it out in inhospitable conditions. You actively thought back to the happy days. You didn't pine and yearn for a pretty girl; you relived the times you'd romped with the best.

'Chopper,' said Huey from the obbo slit, and the image of Sharon, the feel of her, the silky softness of her skin, the soft and crushing warmth of her lips, vanished like a burst balloon. Punch sat up in the hide and was back on West Falkland.

The heli's sound wavered up and down the scale.

'Zig-zagging,' said Ickey.

'And the wind's playing tricks.'

There was no doubt the helicopter was making a methodical search.

If the Argies had infra-red surveillance equipment up there the body heat of the men in their hide could be identified. Punch did not believe there was any IR stuff in the chopper. Had there been such kit he felt the patrols would have been spotted earlier.

After a time the helicopter buzzed away, *chip-chop-chip*, her rotors thrashing away into silence.

'Caldeiro must be doing his nut,' said Dexter with great satisfaction.

Punch went on worrying away at the surveillance problem.

'Next time we get some natural cover overhead. If this bastard Caldeiro has the pull you reckon, Joker, he can fly some IR kit in. A thermal imager will —'

'It'll mostly be Yank kit,' put in Ickey. 'That's good.'

'Check.'

'I don't want to move Dusty and Zeb around too much,' warned Rommel.

'We ought to have them shipped out in good time,' said Punch.

When night drew on they contacted base and received ETA of the chopper. A purposeful air gripped them now. For men superbly trained to a pitch of fighting perfection, to remain hidden in holes in the ground proved an arduous task. They welcomed their release, fully knowing that the moment they'd rested up a trifle they'd be off on another hairy expedition behind enemy lines. This life held a fascination every one of them imbibed, drug-like.

Although they all felt like complaining vigorously when the little helicopter touched down at the RZ, they knew the crew were putting their lives on the line. No one passed too adverse a comment. The fact remained – the chopper would have to make three lifts.

Punch simply told them what was going to happen.

'Rommel and his patrol first, get clear with the wounded. You, SS, will go with them. Second lift Ickey and his patrol, and you, Dingle, with them.'

'But –'

'Leave all the extra kit with the Joker and me. We'll fly out last.'

The pilot, laconic in his bulbous helmet and flying kit draped with cables and lines, agreed on the split, contenting himself with the comment that they'd better get the weights divided up right. He was pushing the limits as it was. The first patrol plus SS lifted off.

Dingle looked as disgusted as SS had been when he boarded. Punch just wouldn't stand still for an argument.

They piled the excess kit in the far end of the hide and

settled down to wait for the return of the chopper. Flying at night over hostile territory – for that was what the Falklands were for the time being – was a tough prospect.

True to form, Dingle tried to argue it out with Punch when the helicopter returned.

'Let 'em take the big Scimitar and all the kit – I'll hang on with you and the Joker –'

'Nope. Leave the wireless here and the kit. You fly out, Dingle. No arguments.'

So the chopper made her second return flight with Ickey's patrol plus Dingle. Punch and Dexter were left in the hide with a pile of kit, the wounded men's weapons, the big Scimitar and ammo. They settled down again, one on one off watch, ready for the last lift before daylight.

The whole operation was timed down to seconds. If daylight caught them too close in, the Argie Air Force would come screaming in to blow them out of the water.

With just the two of them, waiting like this, made Dexter realize afresh how much he valued Punch Fuller. The big fellow was by nature intemperate, impatient, always anxious to get on with it and have a bash. Yet he could sit silently and still, calm with an inner power that impressed Dexter.

The knock on the head had produced some strange – some extraordinary – changes in Punch's actions. He'd apparently gone berserk, he'd tried to strangle his oppo, he'd gone blind. Yet after all that, now he could sit quietly in the hide and wait. Impressive, that was. Dexter felt and knew he could never express those thoughts to Punch.

A distant roaring in the sky snapped their attention into top gear.

Dexter looked out and said: 'Hey, Punch. Look at this!'

Across the shrouded sky a meteor roared and flamed.

Light pulsed down, twisting and spuming in a billowing trail. Against the stars they could just make out a black bat shape.

The streaming tail of flame poured across the sky and vanished into the darkness of the ground.

The concussion racketted about them and vibrated through the earth.

No billowing conflagration followed, no boiling upsurge of orange and black, no mushroom-shaped cloud to mark the destruction of the aircraft.

'Hercules,' said Punch, 'sure of it.'

'They put down in one piece, just about.'

Punch Fuller did not say words to the effect that their duty required them to carry out a reconnaissance. What he did say was, 'Let's mosey over there and take a dekko. If we don't recce, we ain't a recce patrol, are we?'

Chapter Fourteen

Understandably enough, Sam Day expressed scathing contempt for his brother's army friends.

They'd achieved nothing, the seventy-five quid had been handed over at gunpoint, and his front windows had been smashed to perdition. All in all, a negative result for what had been billed as a great victory.

'We're having a whip-round in the unit, Sam,' Dexter told him. 'We'll pay for a new window.'

'I should think so.'

'And we've not forgotten these buggers killed your brother.'

'There's no proof.'

Punch and Dexter and the others accepted that. Harriet and Ernie's parents had to be kept out of it.

'We'll get the law on them, you'll see, Sam, and then –'

'I can't afford to be seen with you lot –'

'Check.'

'So –'

'So we'll handle it their way from now on.'

Soon after Sam cleared off large and craggy men alighted from a battered old Cortina in the hotel car park. They carried golf bags and cricket bags, and capacious suitcases. Sportsmen, they were, quite clearly, and if it was a little difficult to decide just which sport they practiced, no one really noticed. They booked rooms and they were very quiet and soft-spoken, acting as perfect gentlemen.

What was probably their opposing team turned up an hour or so later in a Bedford van. These gentlemen were, also, large and craggy. They also carried golf bags and suitcases. They, too, were most polite and soft-spoken.

Lieutenant Miles Barker was not completely Kojak-bald; but what hairs he had floated wispily here and there upon his cranium. His moustache was large, luxurious and gave his face a most menacing look. In the last tournament within Strike Force he'd only just been beaten at *keninja* by Smyjo, and Smyjo himself had been heard to remark that Barky was getting a trifle warm at unarmed combat.

In the bedroom where they all squeezed in very quietly, Barky started by saying: 'First thing. Once we get this thing under control, we go by the book. We get the law and the police in and let them finish off. No arguments.'

Jock flipped a commando knife up and down in his fist, a little trick of his. His oppo, Trampas, usually spoke for both of them. Trampas was called Trampas because he looked like it. Now he said: 'Once we get it under control.'

Looking around at these dozen men, Dexter was struck by their appearance. Usually when they held a Chinese Parliament to thrash out the operational planning they'd be wearing combat uniform and equipment. Now they wore windcheaters and jackets and jeans. But the most immediately odd effect was the look on their faces. They were sun-tanned, bronzed, tough and craggy, yes. But they were only that. They were not tiger-striped. They were not daubed in ferocious stripes that, whilst adopted for concealment and camouflage purposes, gave their faces that look of incredible ferocity.

Sharply, Barky snapped out, 'The last thing we want in the streets is a gun battle!'

'Oh,' said Spider, reflectively, 'I dunno ...'

'Yeah,' said his oppo, Lawless.

Dexter realized that each bloke would take that yeah to mean what he wanted it to, either way. Interesting ...

Each man accepted a task, and during the rest of the week Punch worked all his charm on the little barmaid. He reported that she knew of this Eddie, that he was bad news, and if all that was said of him was true, then he ought to be locked up for life.

'He bosses his gang,' confirmed Barky. 'My informants indicated he was not associated with any other organized crime outfits. He wiped out a rival gang year or so ago, since then it's been all quiet.'

The new window duly went into the fish parlour. The day for the next collection came around and Dingle and SS went off with their cameras and tape recorders. The rest positioned themselves according to plan.

The tensions were inherent in the situation and did not have to be emphasized. The fraught consequences of the coming confrontation needed no elaboration.

The main party entered Day's Fish Parlour via the back entrance. Harriet and her parents were gently guided outside. The moment he'd flipped the Open/-Closed sign, Sam was escorted outside and effectively silenced. They were gentle but firm, and his frightened eyes glared above the gag. SS and Dingle's equipment was set up in record time, and then the door opened and Eddie and his henchmen entered.

Barky was relieved to see Eddie had come himself, for the chances were he'd delegate this second collection to two-tone shoes Jim. Eddie looked surprised.

'Who the hell are you? Where's Sam?'

Decked out in his apron behind the counter, Barky spread his hands, looking apologetic.

'Gone away. Can I help?'

'Did he leave an envelope for me?'

124

Barky said: 'Are you Eddie, the man who murdered Sam's brother, Ernie?'

That, conceded Dexter, crouched under the counter, was putting the boot in in fine style.

Eddie's immediate reaction should not have surprised anyone. He took out his revolver, shoved it at Barky, and said, 'If you want the same, punk, you're asking for it.'

Blocker surged forward. 'Can I hit 'im now, Mr Eddie?'

'Wait —' Eddie must have realized there was more to this situation. He glared around, but the little dining area was empty. 'If you're one of Ernie's pals, punk, you'll get the same —'

'You mean,' said Barky in that smooth incisive tone of voice, 'you'll push my face into the fish fryer?'

'Yeah! Too right — now hand over the cash or …'

Two-tone Jim yelped: 'Weasel — run outside and —'

'That's it,' said Barky. 'Bring in your men with the sawn-off shotguns. Quite like to make their acquaintance.'

Weasel ran outside. Jock showed him the commando knife — in fact he stuck it in a little way — and Weasel promptly forgot his message. The two shotgun men were staring rather sickly down the barrels of Uzis, held in the fists of Trampas and Pugsy. Diffused street lighting turned the scene into a macabre ballet as the three gangsters were herded rapidly into the Bedford van, where they were tied up with rather less care than that bestowed upon Sam.

Inside the fish parlour Eddie swelled with his own power. He ran these streets and he bossed everyone by methods ancient and evil, methods he had refined to suit himself.

'You've had it, son,' he told Barky. 'No one messes with me.'

He half-turned, waiting for his sawn-off backup.

Barky still wasn't satisfied.

'That revolver you're pushing in my face, Eddie – d'you have a licence for it? And you two,' to Blocker, immense and threatening and two-tone Jim, beginning to jitter at the non-appearance of the gunmen, 'you know, of course, that you're both accessories to murder? In fact, there were two of you involved in killing Ernie. You'll all be topped, one way or another.'

'Where the hell are those two idiots?' shouted Eddie. He swung the revolver about, and then leaned forward to grab Barky by the collar. 'I'll show you if I'm fooling! You're for the fish fryer, punk, if you don't –'

He stopped speaking as the rest of the lads stood up behind the counter. Their armoury really was impressive, Dexter felt, as the line of gun barrels covered the three gangsters.

Barky said: 'We don't want to shoot you. Well, we do want to shoot you for killing Ernie; but we're taking you in to the local police for them to sort you out.'

'And,' added Punch, making a long speech, 'if you give us any trouble *we'll* sort you out.'

Eddie gave a strangled kind of shriek. He dropped the revolver. After a little time in which he and his pals were herded outside, he managed to cough out, 'Who are you bastards? I'll get you for this –'

'Yeah?' said Barky. 'Think again, my son, think again.' The video and audio recordings of Eddie's words were safely with SS and Dingle. No recordings were being made now. 'We're Special Forces. You know what that means. Any trouble from you – *any* trouble – and you're dead.'

Eddie swallowed and remained silent.

Afterwards, when they left the local police station and their records and prisoners had been handed over for processing, Punch let out a wistful sigh.

'I was really lookin' forward to tangling with that

126

Blocker.'

'Leave it out,' Barky told him. 'A nice smooth low-profile operation. The cops have enough to go on. And there'll be no comeback from Eddie. He's scared right down to his underpants.'

Lieutenant Miles Barker had been a police cadet in his younger days before joining the army. He'd picked up some useful tips. Punch nodded; but Dexter saw his oppo was regretting the loss of a little punch-up.

Now, as they looked down on the scene of the Hercules crash on West Falkland, Dexter was ruefully aware that the big fellow still wanted to exercise his muscles in some useful way before pulling out.

The Hercules had ploughed in in one piece, the two engines and wing which were still attached flapped pathetically against the ground, the other wing and the two engines which were on fire had dropped off to be extinguished. The wreck humped there like any old stranded whale, high and dry and finished.

'The Yanks build them Hercs real good,' said Punch.

'Yeh. Can you make out what they're doing? They look like they're all on their knees praying.'

Punch let out one of his nasty little sniggers, saying, 'Getting ready to be chopped.'

He was still itching for a fight. They'd had to abort the third lift, for the chopper would be spotted far too easily and the ship had to clear the shore. Punch made up his mind that this Hercules crash was important. He just knew it was. All the expertise and training helped; but it was Punch's nose for trouble that confirmed the instinctive belief.

The aircraft had been making a night run to the airfield at Port Stanley, something had fouled up with the engines, and she'd crashed here in West. All right. So what was so important that it had to be flown into Port Stanley? It sure as hell wouldn't be tins of baked beans!

Hidden in their lair, with their tiger-striped faces looking down on the crashed C130, Punch and Dexter looked for all the world like wolves glaring hungrily upon the sheep pens, or foxes upon the chicken roosts. In any war there are hard, unpleasant and dirty jobs to be done. These men were the hard, unpleasant and – inevitably out on patrol – dirty men to do those jobs.

They'd found a good obbo spot among rocks in a crest line that formed a ragged semi-circle on the starboard side of the C130. Daylight seeping into the soggy atmosphere showed up everything in a dank silvery-green light that might mist over before it cleared to the brilliance of these unnatural days. With the strengthening of the light, every detail became clearer.

'They ain't praying, they're fixing something to haul the whole side clear – the doors are jammed tight underneath.'

'Yeh.'

The Hercules had been flying something important into Port Stanley airfield. Dexter felt his interest screwing into tension as the Argentines worked; and he forced himself to relax. By the time the Argies hauled out whatever it was – why, then he'd know.

Then, again, perhaps the cargo wasn't all that important. They'd airily dismissed baked beans as being an impossible freight for a C130 to run through to Port Stanley at night; the cargo could be something just as unlikely. Bog paper for the Officers' Mess at the general's HQ, perhaps. The latest films to be shown to the staff, copies of *Gente* hot off the press, a fresh issue of anoraks for the coming winter.

If all this seemed ludicrous, he only had to remind himself of the fish and chip business back home. That seemed ridiculous, trouble over a fish and chip shop. But it was all of a piece with what was going on out here in the Falklands. Someone was trying to rip off someone else, be it islands or cash from the till. Yes, it was all of a piece, and down there in that written-off Hercules was something that was as valuable as the integrity of the proprietor of a fish and chip shop.

The ripping sound of the side coming off reached them clearly. Punch aligned the sights to get the first look.

The light was now good enough for Dexter to see the work going on down there in some detail as Punch peered through his sight. The Argies had made an opening in the side of the aircraft. He doubted if they were the crew, and he found himself oddly hoping the poor devils of Argie airmen had not been killed in the crash. There was altogether too much death floating about down here at the bottom of the world, and whilst it was all too cruelly accurate to say that we are all first cousins to the shovel, unnecessary and wanton death displeased him.

The tail rotor of a small heli showed just beyond the tall fin and rudder of the Hercules, so the Argies had been smartly on the ball. A few sudden crashes from inside the craft were followed by a backward rush by the men working down there.

'Here she comes,' grunted Punch.

They'd rigged up a small derrick with block and tackle and men tailed on to the line. A long cylindrical shape began to angle out of the hole in the fuselage.

'What's that – eight or nine foot long?'

'Yeh. Around.'

'Less than a foot in diameter –'

'Yeh. Container tube.'

'Torpedo – no, no. Missile.'

The men of Strike Force, under the major's goading, swotted up on current military hardware. If you were in their business you had to know your trade. So both men knew what they were looking at.

'The Argies don't have tracked launchers – no. They bung 'em on 6×6s.'

'That's right. This beauty is on her way to Stanley airfield to knock down Harriers.'

The Argentine swung the tube out and gently lowered it to the ground. They worked well and began the operation all over again to bring out the next missile.

'Roland, I'll bet,' said Dexter.

'The Argies have the shelter version, and general opinion has it it ain't as good as Rapier. But it's a SAM, and it works, and if some poor sod of a Harrier pilot gets one up his tail pipe over Stanley –'

'Blooey.'

'Yeh.'

That conversation had been unnecessary, and the consequent ending even more unnecessary. Neither felt the need to add: 'So we have to see the SAMs don't ever reach Port Stanley airfield.'

'The launchers will be in position already. These are fresh rounds, ammunition supply.'

'Yeh.'

As a SAM system, Roland had been developed by Aérospatiale of France and Messerschmitt-Bölkow-Blohm of West Germany under the combined title of Euromissile. They'd sold well to Argentina. That was perfectly all right, for Argentina was an ally in that sense. Like Exocet, Roland was now to be turned on the British.

Punch lowered the sight and said, 'Think I'll work around the back, take a dekko at that little chopper.'

Seeing no need for a reply, Dexter remained silent as Punch wriggled back off the skyline. After that Dexter knew he wouldn't see Punch again until the big fellow reported back; and the Argies most certainly wouldn't spot him.

Dexter spared a thought to wonder what it was like for a pilot out of the Navy or the RAF to sit in the cockpit of a Harrier and go screaming into the attack knowing some Argie blighter had him in his sights, was locking the radar on, and was about to let loose with a Roland SAM.

It couldn't be very pleasant. Maybe you could argue that it was like getting up to charge forward with machine guns pooping off at you; there was a difference in Dexter's book. If you were on good old terra firma and someone shot at you with a machine gun, you could hit the dirt and bury your head and rear portions in the muck. But – in an aeroplane? Nowhere to hide, then. Of course, you could always fire a Very pistol or let rip some chaff to confuse the IR seeker head of the missile. You could – if you flew a VTOL Harrier – viff, carry out a vector in flight so that you went one way and, hopefully, the missile went the other. All the same, feeling for the Harrier pilots, Dexter knew he and Punch had to get shot of those Roland SAMs somehow.

Work continued beside the shattered bulk of the Hercules. The cylinders containing the SAMs were carefully stacked on a bare patch of ground. The light gained and it was going to be another of those unaccountable fine days.

After Dexter had figured out that Punch would have just about had enough time to reach around to the other side, the big fellow came on the air.

'Joker? All correct?'

'Check.'

'Nothin' much doing this side. Not much cover, either. Think I'll – hell, where'd it go?'

'What?'

'Joker – I'm ...'

Dexter waited. Silence rode in over the airwaves.

'Punch. Come in, Punch, for –'

'I'm here.'

'You all right?'

'Sure.'

'Your eyeballs?'

'Twinge of a headache, thass' all.'

Dexter said: 'Git back here, Punch, on the double.'

'All right, all right. Where d'you think I'm going? Have a paddle with Sharon in Fuengirola?'

'Come the day.'

Punch signed off. Dexter stowed the radio. Something had happened. If Punch's eyesight was playing him up again then the future looked suddenly and most decidedly bleak.

The droning sound drifting in from the east strengthened. The chopping clatter of a helicopter buzzed up the scale. Dexter squinted up.

A damned great Chinook flew in, double rotors whirring, and landed neatly beside the wrecked Hercules.

Not long now and those Roland SAMs would be on their way in the capacious belly of the Chinook, flying in to Stanley airfield ready to blow British Harriers out of the air.

Chapter Fifteen

'What the hell happened to you, Punch?'

'Nothing.'

'Yeh?'

'Yeh!'

'Oh, come off it! Your eyeballs went on the blink again.'

'I c'n see your ugly face now, can't I?'

No good fuming at the big fellow's intransigence. If Punch's eyes went back on him now, they'd be in schtuck. But that wasn't the big worry. The big worry was just what had really been done to Punch Fuller by that blow on the head.

As though to confirm that whatever happened on the other side of the wrecked Hercules had reinforced the effects of Punch's injury, his loquaciousness surfaced once again. He snugged down in the hide and looked malevolently upon the Argies and their SAMs.

'We've gotta stop them Rolands. That Chinook won't take long. If we had a few LAWs to slap into 'em —'

'Well, we ain't.'

The 66mm rockets would have demolished the helicopter, and hopefully have blown up the damned anti-aircraft missiles as well.

'Now if it was night time,' went on Punch in that fretful tone of voice, 'we could sneak down and —'

'Wrap it up, Punch! We have no LAWs and it isn't night time.'

'All right, all right!'

Presently Punch said: 'See that turdhead waving his arms about and giving orders? I'm going to plug him. That'll make the others think on.'

'Aspet, aspet! Let's work out a plan first.'

'Mallet the buggers! That's the best plan.'

Horrendous visions of having to tie Punch Fuller down arose before Dexter. In this unnatural mood the big fellow was quite likely to stand up, swivel his Sterling forward and go charging down, hollering like a maniac.

Dexter corrected himself. It was not that the mood was unusual in Punch, for he'd act in this belligerent up-and-at-'em way as part of his normal psychology; rather, it was more the way he carried on and the suspicious talkativeness. Punch went on rambling away to himself, partially under his breath. He was a good enough soldier to know the Joker spoke the sober truth.

'All right, Joker!' he burst out at last. 'We hit the orfizers, we hit the pilot, we hit anybody with a hunk of gold braid about him! Check?'

'That ought to hold 'em, at least for a time.'

'Long enough for the lads to get here.'

Neither of them bothered to worry about how they were to last the day until nightfall, when the heli would fly in for them. Any thought of just skulking and hoping the Argie Chinook wouldn't fly off was out. Right out. Those Rolands had to be stopped. Positive action was therefore required.

The men of Strike Force were rather good at positive action.

The two SLRs levelled. That instant, a pungent whiff, a tasted gust of the smells of vinegar and salt, of fish and chips frying, seared into Dexter. He could smell fish and

chips and salt and vinegar and he could remember what
had happened to Ernie Day. He knew what Eddie's gang
had done, how they'd coerced and overpowered and
forced themselves in where they weren't wanted,
thieving and stealing and murdering. Well, that poor
devil of an Argie in his sights now ... If his greedy and
stupid government hadn't done what they'd done, then
there would be no need to press the trigger with exquisite
skill, and send a round through the poor bastard's brain.

The pilot fell, the officer giving orders fell, and the two
second rounds belted out to claim more victims.

Almost immediately Dexter shifted to the cockpit area
of the big chopper. He felt much better driving bullets
into the windows and smashing the instruments, far
better than shooting other men, despite his intense
feelings on the matter.

Punch tried a mag at the rotor heads, hoping to
damage that notoriously weak helicopter part.

Down there by the Hercules wreck men simply
vanished. One minute they were working away at the
canistered Roland rounds, the next they were noses in
the peat under the nearest bit of cover.

Someone started shooting a rifle off. The rounds went
nowhere. Punch took a careful look, finished up the mag,
and slid back down the damp slope between angular
rocks.

'That oughta foul up the chopper's rotor head.'

'Perhaps. If we're lucky.'

'You questioning my shooting eye, young Joker?'

'Nah.'

Dexter joined Punch. They began to work around
away from that last site to another they'd spotted that
looked useful, about fifty metres away.

'All the same,' said Dexter when they positioned
themselves. 'All the same. Mallet 'em we do. Kill the poor
little devils. All for what? A few miserable islands no

one cares tuppence about.'

'Think of the principle, my son, the principle.'

'Think of the oil and krill, more like. And the kelpers. I suppose it's worth it for them –'

'Sure it is. But it's the principle that matters.'

'You know what you can do with principles, Punch.'

'Well, we had 'em for Ernie Day, didn't we?'

'Yeh. Too right.'

The two situations weren't quite identical, of course. However grandiose the Argentines might believe their occupation of British islands to be, and however farcical it might appear in the context of the giant confrontation between East and West, it was still leagues away in scale from a fish and chip shop racket. In principle, though, it was scaringly similar.

'I'll tell you one thing,' said Punch, comfortably lying on his back, hands behind his head, staring at the sky.

'Wozzat?'

'Old SS and Dingle, and the rest of the lads, are going to be sick they've missed this little punch-up.'

Staring down with his head low beside a boulder, Dexter scanned the wreck, the chopper, the little heli beyond the Hercules. Nothing stirred down there. If they could hold the Argies in place until the British heli arrived with a LAW or two, and some of the lads, then they could settle the hash of those damned Rolands once and for all.

'They'll be here,' he said with perfect confidence.

'Oh, sure. But the Argies aren't going to sit around doing nothing, are they? They'll have to make a move.'

'If they try to charge us –'

Punch's voice sounded grim. 'They'll have to come through two mags of SLR and one of Sterling and one of your Enfield IW. They'll never make it.'

'Nope.'

'I reckon Ickey'll come back with 'em.'

Dexter recalled how Ickey Frost had rebelled when his sobriquet changed from Icey. He'd accepted the change in the end. Then a strapping lad from the Green Jackets had joined, personally selected by the major, called Michael Stanton. He said his name was Mickey.

'Not on,' was the major's decision. 'Mickey and Ickey sound the same. And Ickey is in first. You'll have to be Mike.'

'No, sir!' said Stanton. 'I'm *never* called Mike. Sounds as though I'm always off for a kip – sir.'

'You call me the major. All right. Then you can be Stumer, since you appear to believe you've set me one.'

'Stumer!'

'Make it so!'

So Stumer Stanton joined. He did not wear the red beret of the Paras, and his green one was black enough to have wiped out the inside of a coal hole. SSF did not wear a special beret, in white or beige or whatever; as part of their cover each man continued to wear the head dress of his parent unit.

On patrol they wore a weird assortment of headgear – balaclavas, cloth caps, cap comforters, even a crap hat if the occasion warranted that extravagance. Trampas often wore a wideawake over his balaclava.

An occasional movement flittered momentarily down between the wreck and the Chinook. Dexter didn't bother to shoot when the target was so fleeting. If anybody climbed up into the cockpit of the Chinook he'd drill the poor sod and feel sorry for him as he pressed the trigger.

Slowly the sun passed across the sky. The day remained bright and clear in this somewhat unseasonable weather, for which Punch and Dexter were duly grateful, and their continued observation of the Argentines revealed the predicament the Argies found themselves in.

They had a supply of anti-aircraft missiles to get to

Port Stanley airfeld. Their Hercules had blown two engines and crashed. They'd naturally sent in a heavy-lift helicopter to take the SAMs out, and some maniacal British had shot the chopper up, killed the pilot, and prevented all movement of these vital stores.

There was one obvious answer, and that took a trifle longer to materialize than Dexter had anticipated.

The familiar and – in this context – hateful *chip-chop-chip* of a helicopter's rotors clattered in from the east. The sound rose and fell. It bore on, growing louder and louder.

Punch silently checked the poncho over their hide.

Dexter, executing the same action, reflected that if there was genuinely good IR equipment flying above them they'd have to think again about this anti-surveillance technique.

With an eye to a chink he watched.

Three helis landed, one after the other, near the stranded Hercules and Chinook.

'Now that's stupid,' declared Punch.

'Yeh.'

'They should'a –' began Punch.

'Mebbe not. No one's alighting. They're just getting genned up.'

'Well, we blow 'em up, starting now.'

'Check. They'll spot us, for sure.'

'So?'

'So we blow 'em up.'

Two SLRs, aimed by men used to hitting what they aimed at, lined up on the three newly arrived helicopters.

'Fish in a barrel,' grunted Punch. 'Bleeding fish in a barrel.'

Dexter said nothing, lining up on the perspex canopy of the second chopper, leaving the first to Punch. The third would be a free for all.

Then Punch made one of his rare attempts at a joke.

'Although, Joker, for you it'd be a beef and onion pie in a barrel, yeh?'

'Yeh. Let's go.'

The two rifles cracked as one.

Perspex shattered, flying fish-like shards in the light. The rotors of the helis, which had not stopped revved up, whirling faster and faster. Dexter felt he hadn't scored on the second chopper with that shot, decided to have another crack as he was lined up. He pressed the trigger and let fly. The first heli was roaring now, billowing dirt even in that damp soil. The second heli remained fast. The third's perspex nose erupted, and the craft, attempting to rise, sank towards the ground.

The first heli was off now, spinning away. The second remained fast. The third, after that surging lunge for the peat, lifted, turned, dived low beyond the Hercules.

'Goddammit!' Punch looked exasperated.

The two choppers vanished, going low and fast beyond the wreck and the Chinook. The middle chopper sat on the ground, and slowly her rotors wound down to silence.

'You know how tough it is to knock a chopper down with small arms fire,' said Dexter. 'They look so fragile; but they ain't easy unless you have something with a little bite to it.'

'When the lads get here with the LAWs we'll have the bite!'

Neither man made any attempt to shoot the Argentine soldiers who tumbled out of the helicopter. They made for the cover of the wrecks. Punch and Dexter let them go.

Each man knew there would be more to come.

Once Dexter had made a start on keeping a Commonplace Book. As well as writing down what he considered immortal epigrams invented by himself, he'd pasted in cuttings from newspapers and magazines. One

139

item had tickled his fancy, even then. His parents, like Punch's, were dead and buried – but no forgotten – and he'd had to shift and scrape a bit before he settled down to soldiering.

The cutting that had appealed to his sense of humour contained the simple sentence: 'They made skilful use of the ground.'

That was a stock in trade to Strike Force, naturally.

Punch wanted to strike off for a clump of rocks about a hundred metres or so to their left. Dexter hankered after a less-conspicuous indentation he'd spotted when they'd recced the crest line.

'Those rocks are so obvious they'll never think we picked 'em,' pointed out Punch.

'Yeh, thass right. But –'

'Come on. Let's go.'

There was no arguing with Punch in this mood. It was not a question of rank. Normally, Punch would have taken Dexter's views into consideration and, because of his high opinion of the Joker, have credited them with great weight. Now, he just barrelled on.

The realization hit Dexter afresh that his oppo, Punch Fuller, was like a keg of gunpowder, ready to explode any second.

The new hide proved reasonable and in no time they'd organized, arranged their sparse kit, for the bulk of the equipment had sensibly been left in a secure hide further back, and set up an obbo of the wrecks. Dexter checked out the view, saw that nothing appeared to have happened, and settled down to a watching routine. Punch lay on his back, put his hands behind his head and thought of the way Sharon took off her nightie.

Sharon was a big girl, well-built. She'd have to be really, to keep up with Punch. The hotel bedroom they were brazenly sharing under the names they'd been christened with afforded a suitable level of luxury.

Sharon, with blonde hair, a big bust, a waist of curvaceous voluptuousness, and eyes bright with mischief, drew the virulently orange nightie up with artful precision.

'Marks and Sparks,' she said, tauntingly.

'Nothing wrong with their kit.'

'Their what?'

'You heard.'

The openness of Sharon pleased Punch. The orange nightie ascended past rounded thighs, for it had started well above the dimpled knees, past a succulently domed stomach, past breasts that were the real thing without rubber and cantilever supports, past smooth shoulders – and was finally whipped up and chucked down on the bed with some speed.

He started to leap on Sharon, and she said, 'I saw you giving that girl in the bar the eye, I saw.'

'What girl?'

'You needn't be clever! I saw you – and she looked a nice girl, too.'

Punch knew exactly who she was talking about. He'd looked over to check Patsy, who was laughing at some quip the Joker had made, and both men studiously ignored each other. They were in Fuengirola for more than a carefree holiday.

'So I looked at a girl. I'm looking at you, now, Sharon. There's a difference.'

'Oh?'

'Sure. You don't have any clothes on.'

'Oh!'

Then he leapt on her.

When they were lying in each other's arms, panting breast to breast, he said: 'That was just for starters.'

'You –'

'Next time, it's from the top of the wardrobe for you, my girl.'

She laughed at that and tweaked the hairs on his chest, which made him jump. He rolled her over, ready to apply palm to cheek, and was so entranced by pink roundness that he kissed instead of slapping.

At one point in what the poets called their amorous converse Sharon did say: 'I'm still not sure I like Fuengirola, Punch. Really wanted to go to Marbella —'

'Prices a bit fierce there.'

'I know. But —'

'We're taking a trip along there tomorrow. All arranged. See the millionaires at play.'

Sharon Wheeler might be a big girl with long blonde hair and a glamorous figure, and she might be preoccupied with keeping her body beautiful; she was not daft enough to expect a chap like Punch Fuller to be able to afford millionaire living. She liked Punch; sometimes she wished she didn't. Her career of beauty queen/model/film star proceeded far too slowly for her liking and she had to keep herself from panicking as the days ticked by. Here she was, twenty-three years old — old! — she was getting ancient, and still she'd done no more than win a few competitions and pose for a few proper modelling jobs. When she had to pose topless she knew she'd be over the hill as far as her career was concerned.

So she snuggled up to Punch, and told herself that next time she'd pick the fellow to set her career going — at twenty-three years of age she felt nearly past it. Just this last self-indulgent fling with Punch, and then back to finding the money men ...

Lying on the bed with the sweetly-perfumed form of Sharon in his arms, Punch had a vague idea of the way she regarded their relationship. She had ambitions. She knew what she wanted. He'd never earn the kind of money required to keep her in the affluent circumstances to which she aspired.

Still, whilst it lasted, it was good. Like all the men of Strike Force, he'd fobbed her off with some casual story about the way he earned his living, for they all told their girls packs of lies. She knew that he was in the army; just what he did remained obscure.

Perhaps, one of these fine days, he'd take off with a group of his oppos and go for the mercenary life. It didn't really appeal; if that was one way to keep Sharon around that – possibly – might be worth considering.

So, lying now without the soft and firm naked body of Sharon alongside him, he stared up sightlessly at the concealing ponchos as the Joker Dexter kept watch.

They'd kept those damned Rolands stuck on the ground for a goodly time; the day was running out. A few more hours would see the British chopper come clip-clopping in and risking the lives of all aboard. The landing would have to be perilously close to the Argies. There'd be little time once night fell.

Dexter said, 'They're creeping about down there as though there's something on.'

With a resigned grunt, Punch rolled over, shoved up to squint through the gap. Figures flitted between the wreck of the Hercules and the damaged Chinook.

'What th' hell are they up to?'

'Search me.'

'Those other two choppers,' said Punch, with conviction.

'Yeh. Probably. Get in behind us.'

What Dexter did not say was that he felt pretty certain that Captain Hector Caldeiro would heave up very soon to take charge. When that happened the whole situation would change.

Leaving Punch to continue the obbo of the aircraft he swivelled around and settled to check the rear arcs.

The feeling he experienced had to resemble what a piece of cheese felt like in a mousetrap.

Put yourself in the opposition's shoes ...

All right, then. What would Caldeiro do now?

He'd bring the choppers around in a wide circle and land them far enough back so that the troops aboard could disembark without being shot up. Then he'd extend a scouting line and move carefully forward, like a line of beaters flushing the game for the guns. H'm ... So – what was the counter to that? He and Punch would be trapped between the line of beaters and the troops by the wreck. Cheese, all right, in a sandwich.

They'd have to work their way out of it, that was clear enough. Question was – best way out and best way out?

Tactically, the best way out was probably the obvious one.

Directionally, the best way out, left or right, was a matter of ground, of cover, of the lay of the land.

Punch said, 'Sweet FA in the way of cover where I was over on the other side. We'll have to quadrant the Herc and tuck in on the end of the crest line.'

Cautiously, Dexter said, 'D'you spot any decent cover there?'

'Bit.'

'Well, then, mebbe the other way would be –'

'What, Joker? Better the devil you don't know than the one you do?'

'You're calling the shots.'

'Just off the end of the crest there was a gulley.'

'Check.'

With that settled all they needed was a viable excuse to shoot down at the Argie positions. That was not long in coming. Something certainly was taking place down there, for the occasional glimpse of an Argie anorak flitting between C130 and Chinook indicated heightened activity. Neither Punch nor Dexter doubted the courage of the Argentines. If you stopped to think about it, you had to feel sorry for the poor blighters trapped into this

144

invasion business, bamboozled by their government and about to be malletted rotten. When the time for action came the Argies would put up a good scrap, that was the general feeling. Of course, poor devils, they'd lose hands down; but then, that was the way of harsh reality.

A round helmet incautiously showed itself for just too long. Punch loosed off and, instead of simply shooting once – which was all that was necessary – he banged away four rounds. The helmet rolled away from the soldier, whose black-haired head rested on the ground, turned brim up and rocked gently back and forth.

Instantly, return rifle fire blatted in. Bullets cracked and splattered against the rocks, and white chips flew.

'Nice one, Punch.'

'Yeh. Time for the off.'

Keeping low and out of sight below the crest line, they scuttled around the ragged semi-circle of higher ground.

Dexter kept looking back over his shoulder to check the rear. Just how long the choppers would be he couldn't guess; but if Caldeiro had entered the picture then they wouldn't be long. Punch's extravagant rifle-fire had fixed their position on the crest for the Argies. If the plan worked then Caldeiro would land his troops and send them forward to beat the British away from the crest and down onto the waiting guns below – and the Brits wouldn't be there. The cheese in the trap would miraculously have taken wing and flown.

That was the plan.

That sleek bastard Eddie who'd killed Ernie Day had taken wing and flown, too. He'd been all nicely wrapped up by the police, a confession from Blocker to save his own neck giving a certain conviction. Blocker had just hit Ernie. Eddie had shoved his face into the fish fryer and killed him.

And then he'd taken off from the police van on the way to the court, a couple of stocking-masked heavies, pick-axe helves smashing down, a shotgun blast – and he was away.

Well, they sussed out where he'd gone. Spain. Out there he could laugh, take the mickey, relax, extradition laws could fulminate in vain. Oh, yes, Eddie had played it beautifully.

And so did Captain Hector Caldeiro.

Two helicopters must have disgorged their soldiers, ready for the sweep line to form and push the Brits out of their hiding place. Dexter spotted the dark blots of the men out there across the camp.

Punch said: 'Fifty yards or so, Joker. Then we go invisible.'

Before he'd finished speaking a third heli floated up over the edge of rocks, rotors a flashing disc of steel in the light, and streaked low over the sparse vegetation straight for them.

In only moments, exposed there on the sloping hillside with its orange-green vegetation and its whitish-grey rocks, Punch and Dexter would be spotted and the machine guns would open up mercilessly, cutting them down as they ran.

Chapter Sixteen

Bloody Punch Fuller and his incessant chattering!

Punch Fuller was turning into a right wally!

Jack Dexter hurled himself into, under, all mixed up with a straggly bush. Punch went headfirst into its mate. If their boots stuck out, their bottoms upended, they might be spotted. Peaty soil tanged into Dexter's nostrils, the dankness of it all enclosed him clammily. He tried to put himself into a foetal ball and at the same time burrow deeply into the inhospitable ground.

He was well aware that his eyes were glaring madly from his tiger-striped face, his lips ricked back in mingled anger and terror. What a foul up!

The downblast of wind, the flogging of the bush about him, the roaring clamouring through his ears into his head, the sheer overpowering hostility of it all swamped over Jack Dexter, and he felt the presence of the helicopter as a personal nemesis above him. He cringed. He held himelf into himself, and waited for the scything swathe of machine gun bullets to chop him in half.

The noise battered all about him, lifted, dwindled, faded, droned away as the helicopter bore on along the ridge.

Punch was completely unrepentant.

He called across to Dexter in that penetratingly soft whisper: 'Didn't see us, the narner. Told you so!'

Dexter ground his lips together, trapped between his teeth, and made no reply.

'Well?'

Punch was elated, riding a high, his system no doubt drenched with adrenalin.

Eventually, Dexter got out, 'That lot behind us'll be here soon. We'd better find a better hole.'

'Check.'

When they arrived up at Punch's gulley Dexter was not too enamoured of it as a hide; but they went on for twenty metres or so and discovered a little slide where they could spread the ponchos and so give the impression that the slide was just that much bigger. In the space between ponchos, ground and the real slide they constructed their lair.

'Like the time we went after Colonel Gunjepoo,' said Punch, shifting about, talking, checking, generally acting like a mother hen. He was beginning to make Dexter worry, really worry in a frightening way. This was never Punch Fuller.

'Oh, him.' Gunjepoo was not the colonel's real name; Strike Force had the happy habit of bestowing a variety of nicknames upon those with whom they came into contact. Anyway the name suited the colonel. 'For Pete's sake, Punch, sit still!'

'What? Yeh – check – right.'

The third heli had sprung up from nowhere, flying low and hard and on them in a twinkling. Her blades chip-chop-chipped faintly. With an eyeball screwed to a gap in the poncho edge Dexter followed the chopper's progress. The dratted thing was making a careful search of the area where the Brits had shot up the Chinook. Over on the other side there was no sign of the Argie soldiery advancing.

'Won't be much longer now.' Punch spoke in that odd way of his that so terrified Dexter. 'The lads will bring in a few rockets and we'll mallet them Rolands good and proper.'

They ate a few mouthfuls of food, cold and tasteless, and sipped carefully at the water, and dozed on and off by rota.

Their alertness remained sharp so they were fully on the ball when the first Argie showed up on the crest line.

Still as mice hiding from a cat, the two Strike Force men watched the approaching hostiles. Unlike a poor little mouse, they could fight off any cat – unless there were just too many of them. The Argies moved slowly and, by their actions, showed they were checking every indentation and pile of rocks in their path.

At this distance Dexter had no way of knowing if Captain Hector Caldeiro really was in command of this search party, although at a shrewd guess it seemed likely. When the line closed in the blight might show himself. Dexter licked a harsh tongue over raspy lips.

The number of soldiers involved was not great. The two helicopters had done sterling work in bringing this party in. So it was that the centre of the line anchored on the position Punch and Dexter had occupied and spread out to each flank. Studying the hostiles, Dexter saw with satisfaction – and with an emotion he guessed to be relief – that the nearest fellow would cut across the ridge some distance from the end, some further distance from the lair. Splendid!

He swivelled his eyes to glance at Punch. The big fellow lay there rigidly, his immobility remarkable in so energetic a man; and Dexter also saw the way Punch's jaws ground together and guessed he was fighting his new irrational urge to talk.

The line of Argie soldiers moved on, crested the ridge and began to descend. Only moments later they were out of sight. Dexter kept on looking, seeing the small group of officers and NCOs following up, a supernumerary

149

rank. He couldn't decide if one of those dark figures was Caldeiro. Well, it didn't really matter – not now, anyway. As the weather closed in and distances grew tricky and the shadows dropped down, Jack Dexter felt in his bones that he'd run across Hector Caldeiro again.

After a time Punch couldn't hold his tongue still any longer.

'They've gotta be near enough the Herc and the Chinook by now to know they've missed us.'

'Yeh.'

'So what do they do?'

'My best guess is they'll reason we've cleared off. After all, that's the sensible course, right?'

Punch let his nasty little laugh erupt. 'For some, my son, for some!'

'And it's almost dark now. Don't reckon they'll fancy patrolling out in the camp now.'

'I read you loud and clear.'

When darkness dropped down and the temperature with it, the men from Strike Force could go about Strike Force business. This operation represented the kind of work at which they were past masters. Using that lovely little crest to give cover and to shield them from observation from the Argie positions, they circled around and popped up an eye to survey what might be going on.

As Q had reminded them the Argentine night vision equipment being American supplied, was very good. You couldn't just stand up and take a dekko; some little Argie sod'd have you in his sights in no time flat.

Down there the Argies had evidently moved in in style. They were making a real camp of it. No doubt the vino would start flowing. And there'd be sentries out ...

Spanish folk liked and appreciated fine wines. The sun

150

of the Costa del Sol, burning and crisping everything, activated the thirst muscles. They'd drink rotgut if that was all that was available. Punch and Sharon, Dexter and Patsy, went on the trip to Marbella and the two men took no notice of each other. The two girls tended to bristle from time to time, and Punch realized that he hadn't been careful enough. As for Marbella, they saw the millionaires – or quasi-millionaires – at play and they looked much like anybody else. This was intended to be a recce patrol. This was intelligence gathering. It didn't work out like that.

'I'm glad we didn't stay here,' said Patsy, 'no matter what the girls in the office say. I'm glad I thought of coming here.'

Dexter nodded, happy to let pass his own cunning implantation of the Fuengirola destination in her pretty head.

The girls had their hearts set on visiting the yacht marina, where the millionaires sported which was at Puerto Banus. There was almost a hitch when they discovered they would be travelling together, so Dexter took the plunge.

Introducing himself to Punch, he said, 'Seems silly not to join up, you know, strangers in a foreign land.'

Punch played up well, and by the time it was all sorted out a marked lessening of the ice between the girls gave the men some respite. After all, cloak and dagger stuff had to be planned and carried off with panache.

And then they spotted Eddie entering a restaurant.

Just like that. The recce patrol had finished; now it was malleting time.

Down in the chill darkness of a Falklands night malletting time also approached. Punch's Scimitar awoke to life and Dingle's voice rode in.

'Punch?'

'Yeh. Come on in.'

Directions were given and received and soon the shadowy figures of SS, Dingle and Ickey Frost showed up. They were humping kit.

'Got the LAWs?' demanded Dexter.

'Yeh. And better'n that. Got a Charlie G here.'

'We're in business!'

'Grenades, plastic?' queried Punch.

'All here,' confirmed Ickey.

'You been having fun?' said SS.

'You could say that.'

'Sorry to spoil your fun, Punch,' said Dexter. He spoke with deadly seriousness, meaning every word. 'There won't be time for grenades and plastic. That bastard Caldeiro will see to that.'

If Punch Fuller got it into his barbaric head that his oppo the Joker Dexter was implying that Punch would be stopped by some Argie squit, then the keg of gunpowder might explode on the spot. Punch pulled in his lower lip, and then, with a twist to his lips, said: 'Yeh. Still, it was a thought. And if we stand with our ends hanging out like this, the bird will have flown the coop.'

Pointing out the Hercules and the Chinook to the new arrivals was easy enough. The pile of SAMs remained *in situ* and the Argies had thrown over a canvas sheet to keep off the damp. Setting up those things was a devil of a business, and damp could ruin all the delicate electronics. Ickey made a tiny *kekking* sound in his throat.

'Bags the Charlie G. Into that pile – and blooey!'

'Better them going blooey than a Harrier.'

'Too right.'

They sorted themselves out. Punch snaffled a LAW, as did Dexter, whilst Dingle agreed to act as Ickey's Number Two and load the Charlie G. The Carl Gustav

84mm recoilless rifle anti-tank launcher would squirt a voluminous tail of fire. Prudence dictated somewhat rapid redeployment during firing.

Dexter's grim warning proved only too true. Now the Argies were freed from the stinging torment of British rifle fire that had pinned them down, and – no doubt – now that Caldeiro had arrived, they were moving. If the Chinook and the other helis were grounded, then Caldeiro would shift the Roland rounds out in the smaller choppers, a few at a time. This activity now presented itself as Strike Force lined up.

'I always did like a few nice big bangs,' and Punch licked his lips and slanted the 66mm rocket launcher tube down evilly. 'Right – lettem have it!'

The recoilless rifle and the rockets combined to create a tremendous racket, blasting across the boggy ground below the crest. SS cut loose with a long string of fire. In the way of Strike Force, he had possessed himself of a Heckler und Koch HK33. Shooting 5.56mm rounds, the HK33 SS he had snaffled had a forty round magazine and folding butt. He was as proud of it as a kiddy of his new toy at Christmas.

The explosions around the Roland rounds and the slashing rifle proved too much for the Argies preparing to load the SAMs into the helicopters. They just ran for it, which was both sensible and helpful.

The Chinook exploded, fuel fires coruscating upwards. The sheeted pile of Rolands erupted skywards, and still Ickey slammed the rounds out. Dingle was hard at it, swinging the venturi and loading, and letting Ickey understand that he was ready to shoot again.

Using LAWs this close in meant that Strike Force were perilously close. They did not concern themselves with that. Those Rolands had to be prevented from reaching Port Stanley airfield and being used to shoot down Harriers.

'That's it,' yelped Punch. He quite obviously wanted to go on shooting; but he'd expended all his LAWs and the site below them was a sea of flames. It was clearly time to go.

'And bring the Charlie G!' snapped Ickey. 'I signed for that!'

'Don't fash yourself. over that,' Dingle told him. 'They're chucking the old Charlie G out and dishing out the LAW80.'

'Get moving!' snarled Punch. Once he'd made up his mind to clear off he wanted no shilly-shallying. They melted away from the fiery reflections and vanished into the concealing darkness. That darkness would not hide them from sophisticated night sights unless they'd gone invisible. No chance of that – not with the chopper waiting for them ...

Once they were back over the crest line they could dip down into its concealment and breathe a little easier.

Now they had to make a quick hack to the chopper, lugging Ickey's signed-for Charlie G between them. On the way they'd picked up the rest of the kit stowed by Punch and Dexter.

In the final moments of this patrol they had to carry burdens of equipment with them; in the blinding sunlight of Spain they had to carry the burden of two delectable girls ...

'Look, Mr Dexter,' said Punch with the formality of the newly-introduced. 'Why don't you go over there and buy ice creams all round? I must go and water the horses.'

Patsy laughed, and Sharon stared haughtily at Punch. He squinted up his eyes in the sunshine and made a face, nodding towards the restaurant where Eddie had vanished.

'All right, but don't be long!' Sharon, too, laughed.
'I won't.'

Dexter felt a fuming helplessness. Punch had done it again. They were going to snaffle this toe-rag Eddie and take him back to England. Q would arrange transport somehow. Now Punch was off and running solo. Dexter watched in impotent fury as Punch strode rapidly to the restaurant, clearly a man looking for a lavatory.

Under the striped awning Punch tried the door and found it locked. The restaurant was not open yet. Nevertheless, Eddie had gone somewhere. Maybe the turdhead had an interest in the place – that was quite likely. Punch started off around the side looking for the back door.

As he reached the corner of the building two girls walked out of the rear doorway, taking no notice of him, chattering away in voluble Spanish. He waited a couple of heartbeats and then sidled up to the open door and looked in.

Beyond a tiny space containing nothing apart from a broom and bucket he could see Eddie gesticulating away in the kitchen, talking to a swarthy, frizzle-haired fellow in a monkey suit. The waiter nodded, turned and went off towards the front of the restaurant. Punch whistled in the first door, carefully avoided both bucket and broom, looked into the kitchen.

The smells of the place, spicey and exotic, tickled his nostrils. The broad tables, pots and pans shining, the array of cooking implements, all looked normal. The stoves were alight. Eddie was staring about like some king surveying his dominion. Punch walked in very sedately.

Eddie did not hear the man from Strike Force until Punch took him by the back of the neck and shook him like a rabbit.

'I ain't going to kill you, Eddie, like you murdered my

155

pal Ernie Day. But you're coming back to Blighty with me and they'll put you away for a long time.'

The speech from Punch represented pent-up force exploding. He held Eddie easily enough. Eddie made a mistake.

Shaken by the neck though he was, shattered by this ambush, he contrived to pull a natty little automatic from his pocket. He tried to turn it so that he could shoot Punch in the guts. That was, indeed, a most serious mistake.

Punch Fuller didn't really hit him. He just bashed him over the back of the head with his free hand. He let go. Eddie staggered forward, slumping, dropping the auto, feet tangling helplessly.

Punch watched him fall.

Outside, Jack Dexter fretted. He bought two ice creams at the little kiosk and then said, 'I need to, as well ...' and without giving the girls time to argue took off for the restaurant. He found the door locked, reached the corner, saw Punch running out of the back door.

Dexter could see, etched in his mind as he hacked along on West Falkland, that picture of his oppo running up the alley ...

Now Punch led on with vigour. The chopper pilot waited where he said he'd wait. The rendezvous came up neatly, and Dexter, for one, felt relief.

'Get aboard,' said Punch.

As he finished speaking fire broke out in their rear and livid streaks of flame scythed the night. Bullets began to crack and spit about the men. The helicopter, a dark mass against the darkness, rang with hits.

'Get in! Get in!'

Ickey and Dingle fairly threw the Charlie G in, SS slammed in the big Scimitar, jaguar packs fell into a heap in the heli's cabin. Ickey leapt aboard, grabbed Dingle's hand. Bullets clattered past. SS heaved Dingle up, jumped in. Dexter followed, crouching by the door to look back.

The chopper would be perfectly visible through the Argie night sights. They were shooting a devil of a lot of stuff. The engine picked up, roaring, and the rotors turned.

Dexter looked back.

'Come on, Punch!'

Punch ran for the chopper. Dexter saw him. Weirdly superimposed over that picture of his oppo running for the helicopter in the Falklands he could see Punch running down the alley in sunny Spain. He blinked. Punch ran down the alley, face set, breathing through his nose.

'What happened?'

'The turdhead – he fell down. Fell with his face in a vat of frying oil ...'

The chopper's noise drowned out thought. Drowned memory. If the similarities in the two situations were obvious, the differences were just as startling. Punch stopped running for the helicopter. He stopped stock-still. Dexter could see bullets churning up the damp ground. A couple of rounds slapped through the cabin. In only moments someone would be hit, the pilot would be killed ...

'*Punch*! Come on!'

The chopper was lifting, was slowly rising away from the murderous fire.

'Joker! *I can't see!*'

That was what Punch's mouth formed, those words, unheard in the racket of the engine and the blades. Ickey yelped, suddenly, in astonishment.

'I've been hit.'

Punch held a hand out, feeling the air. A bullet flicked

his anorak. So turdhead Eddie had ended up with his face in a fish fryer, just like Ernie; maybe he didn't die of it, maybe he did. But Punch Fuller was going to die, *now* ...

Gripping onto his Enfield IW, Dexter screamed into the cabin.

'Take her up! *Go, go!*'

The pilot responded, even if he didn't hear, and the helicopter began to lift. Dexter swung his legs over the coaming of the door, poised, pushed, jumped.

He landed on the peaty soil soggily, knees bent. The enormous rush of wind blattered him. The entire world, or so it seemed, was one smashing concussion.

The helicopter was precious and had to be preserved.

But one man of Strike Force wasn't going to abandon his oppo to the likes of Captain Hector Caldeiro.

As the chopper lifted up and away to safety, Jack the Joker Dexter put his head down and started towards Punch Fuller. He didn't have a white cane. But, somehow, they'd get out of this one, together.

You didn't get into Strike Force easily, and in these circumstances, by God, you wouldn't leave easily, either.